Falling
for a
Monster

Delilah Hunt

Meiki Rhule, thanks for your help and vote of confidence on my book. To Theodora Taylor, the Queen of IR Romance, you are truly a wonderful and supportive lady. Thanks to all of my readers who have welcomed me back to the world of publishing. You guys are the best.

Contents

Prologue

Thirteen Years Ago

Chase was supposed to be hunting. Right now, his blade should've been dripping with blood. From which animal? It didn't matter. It could've been from the wild boar he'd been intent on finding, or better yet, the fat niglet who'd ran from him, causing both of them to land right on their asses in a sinkhole that had loosened near the thick roots of a tree.

Instead of heading home to show off his kill, he was forced to breathe the same air and share the same space as that creature sitting inches away from him.

Larke. That was her name. And of all the stupid names he'd ever heard, hers had to be the worst. Chase wasn't sure how long they'd been inside the muddy sinkhole, just that it was way too long, since she was no longer cringing away from him even though he still had his knife.

Curling his lips, he canted his head and scowled at the girl, trying to figure out why she thought telling him her name would make a difference.

As if he cared! In fact, he didn't know why she'd even started talking to him. Larke was ugly with boring dark eyes and tight curly hair that was held in what he guessed was supposed to be pigtails, although they didn't hang. Worse, around her neck, she had on a fake pearl necklace. He knew it was fake because the beads were much shinier and plastic-like than the ones he'd seen on those rich ladies him and Gramps had eaten dinner with in Alabama last winter.

Chase shook his head with disgust. Dark as she was, he hoped she'd soon begin to blend in with the dirt that matched her nasty skin color. Then he'd be able to concentrate in peace and try to find a way out of this situation.

He scratched his head while eyeing the approaching night's sky. Fuck. There were too many clouds in the sky for his liking. Big fat puffy clouds, that looked as if they were waiting for the right opportunity to burst open and drench the ground with weeks of pent up rainwater. If that happened… Chase squeezed his eyes shut. It wouldn't rain. Wouldn't, he reassured himself. And if it did someone would find him before it began to pour.

He glanced at the girl again. Someone would find *them,* he thought angrily. When everyone found out he'd been so close to a stinkin' nigger he'd definitely be in for a beating.

"Do you think it'll rain before anyone finds us?"

"Don't talk to me," Chase snapped. Moron couldn't even tell when someone was ignoring her. She rolled her eyes then glanced at the book bag beside her foot. He ground his teeth and went back to ignoring her.

Should've killed her before we fell in.

He'd tried, though, hadn't he? And that was what led to all of this—the two of them trapped here; about to spend the night in the cold with the possibility of storm showers beating down on them and worse.

After Chase spied her standing near the woods, on property she'd had no business being on, he'd reached for his knife and took off after her. Despite looking like she'd eaten too much candy and ice cream when her parents weren't watching, she was a fast runner. She'd screamed for him to leave her alone while pounding the moss-covered ground.

He hadn't. How could he, when she was intruding on their land? Just like that chink reporter who'd come sneaking around his grandfather's office last month. Chase had been determined to mete out his own justice to the little intruder. But once he'd caught a hold of her shirttail, everything else happened within a blur. One moment he was running on solid ground, the next his feet were sliding from beneath him in mud with the girl's screams echoing in the woods as they landed inside the sinkhole.

Tired of standing now, Chase sank to the cold damp ground as far away from Larke as humanly possible—which meant there was a tiny space between his shoulder and hers. He groaned inside his eleven-year-old head while sneaking a peek at her reaching down into her bag. She pulled out a candy bar and then another. Hunger and jealousy gnawed at his empty stomach. She had something to eat and he didn't.

He turned his head, hating her even more. Probably thought she was better than him. She wasn't, he reminded himself. As everyone in Lee's Fortress would say: *If the color ain't right...* Well her color wasn't right. That alone made him superior. Among other things. *Lots* of other things that she was probably too dumb to understand.

Reminded of his pride, Chase puffed out his chest, determined to ignore the faint scent of chocolate and peanut wafting in the air. He was doing good, until out of nowhere, something hit him on the leg. Jaws clenched, he jerked his head, teeth bared, intent on reminding her that he was one step away from finishing what he'd started earlier. And he wasn't the least bit afraid of getting into trouble because she was black and absolutely no one would care what happened to her.

He said nothing, however. There was no need. Chase felt the anger drain right out of him as he spied the candy bar beside his foot. The one Larke had tossed his way. The urge to reach for it, tear the wrapper open and stuff it inside his mouth ate at him. His stomach growled, a not so subtle reminder that he'd left home all day, after eating only a bowl of cereal sometime near midday and it was now nearing night.

Leaving the candy in the spot it landed, Chase stared back up at what was definitely storm clouds rolling in. He had no doubt the girl's family was searching for her. As for his family... He wasn't sure. Maybe they hadn't noticed he was missing. When he'd left the house earlier, his mother and stepfather Trevor had been arguing. She'd grumbled again about being tired of housework and too many other things for Chase to remember. His grandfather was somewhere in Louisiana meeting with important people, who were afraid to be seen with him in public but were glad he'd founded Antebellum Resistance. AR, as they called it, was a group that wanted to help make life better for white people since the government was favoring everyone else. Gramps said things would be a whole lot better if America went back to more traditional ways and that included the coloreds being put in their place once and for all.

Everyone needed a place, Chase supposed. Last month his place had been to follow orders and clean up blood, without backtalk or questions. He curled his fingers into a fist and fought the wave of nausea inside his stomach that made him want to throw up. It happened every time he recalled the sound of the bullet cracking the reporter's skull.

The blood splattering on the wall and the scent of bleach they'd used afterward. He'd been forced to watch his grandfather shoot the man after they'd caught him lurking around, peering through a window of AR's main office. His grandfather and Trevor had then convinced the reporter to come inside. There'd been promises of an interview in the privacy of the basement. They had told him he'd learn all about white supremacy and the ins and outs of their neo-Confederate movement that was headquartered in the small town of Lee's Fortress, North Carolina.

"Aren't you going to eat the candy?" The girl's annoying voice cut into his thoughts. She was staring at him, frowning. "Maybe the sugar will put you in a better mood."

Chase turned his head ever so slowly, glaring at her. She shrugged and reached for the candy, pushing it out to him. "Here take it."

Simply because he was so damn hungry and irritated that he was still thinking about what happened last month like a wimp or fairy, Chase snatched the wrapper, making sure not to touch her hand. He bit into the Snickers candy, unsure at first what it would taste like, but uncaring because it meant his stomach would no longer be empty.

After taking the first bite and liking it, he turned to Larke and asked, "Are you fat because you eat this type of stuff all the time?"

"That's not a nice thing to say." She gazed at the ground then lifted her head. "I don't eat candy all day long. I um... Sometimes I eat pizza and bacon too." She snapped her chin up and tossed her head to the side. Now *she* was ignoring him. Whatever. He was happy she finally got a clue... Until he saw her dip her hand in the bag again. This time she had pulled out even *more* candy than before. How was that possible?

His stomach rumbled at the sight of all the sugary treats he was never allowed and had never tasted. Why did she have so many and did her parents actually allow her to eat all of it?

She moved to face him, her eyes narrowed. "I really should let you sit there and starve for everything you did to me today, including calling me a monkey baby before you went insane and came after me with a knife you probably stole from your daddy." She stuck out her chin again. "But you're lucky I'm not as mean as you are." She dropped a handful onto his lap.

Chase ignored her at first, simply staring at his sugary stash meant to ward off hunger. Then before he could stop his big mouth from talking, he asked, "Why do you have so much candy?"

"Birthday party," she said, mouth stuffed with chocolate. "A girl in my class brought them in to share with everyone. Don't they do that at your school? At my old school, I brought in cupcakes for my class. My mom and I baked them together." She touched her necklace. "I also got this for my birthday."

He didn't care about her stupid necklace. Now was his chance to make her jealous. "I don't go to school," he said smugly. "My mom teaches me when the mood strikes her. Or I teach myself sometimes. Real useful stuff too."

She frowned. "Don't you ever get bored?"

"No." It was a lie. Sometimes the boredom drove him crazy. Still, it wasn't that bad, because he *did* get to sneak time in to improve his carving skills, whenever his mother left him alone to learn math and all the other subjects he hated. Other times, Chase was too busy hanging out and driving across states with his grandfather, learning the important things he needed to know. Gramps had even said one day Chase would be the one in charge of AR and everyone in Lee's Fortress would respect and depend on him to help preserve their strong Confederate heritage. He was looking forward to that day when everyone would listen to him.

As for now, Larke seemed satisfied with his answer and had somehow managed to keep her mouth shut for a couple of minutes. Chase rubbed his hand along the sleeve of his shirt. The temperature had begun to drop. He wondered if that was her reason for not talking anymore. Not that he minded. Wasn't like he was getting used to her yapping, or anything foolish like that.

He watched her reach into her wonder bag again. This time she pulled out a yellow sweater that he guessed belonged to her mom because it was much too big and long for her. The sweater was definitely for someone older than a... It suddenly hit him he had no idea how old she was, only that she had to be younger than him. Didn't matter, he reminded himself. He hadn't asked or planned on asking for her age.

Instead of putting on the sweater as he'd expected her to, Larke threw it over her chest and held out one side. She was silently inviting him underneath it. Chase hesitated for all but a second before grabbing a hold of the sweater and scooting closer while pulling his section up to his neck. Maybe if he was braver and tougher he would've turned down her offer, but freezing didn't seem like it would prove anything at all. So he held himself as still as possible, trying not to accidentally brush up against her. When that proved impossible, mainly because of her constant fidgeting, he lowered his head, determined at least to not make eye contact with her.

Some time later, they pushed the sweater away to stand and call out into the night, hoping that whoever was out there searching for them might be close enough to hear. When that failed and their cries were met by the hooting of an owl and the distance grunt of deer deep inside the woods, both sank back to the ground with their knees drawn up, huddled beneath the big sweater.

"I hope it doesn't rain," she said, worried.

"Me too."

His honesty must have awakened the chatter bug inside her because soon she was starting up again. In no time at all Chase had learned that Larke and her mother had recently moved to North Carolina from Missouri after her parent's divorce. Even worse, when she'd asked him about his family, he hadn't hesitated to tell her all about them, including his father who had died in a car crash on his way home late one night.

There was a long stretch of silence before Larke finally said anything to him again. "Now I know why you said those mean things and tried to..." She let the sentence hang and Chase was glad. Because if she tried to make him feel guilty he'd more than likely end up saying other things she *definitely* wouldn't want to hear. Like how one day life would go back to the way it used to be, when people like her would stay in their own neighborhoods and everything would be separated again. Gramps said since people didn't like hearing talks of slavery and because it made neo-Confederates look bad if they discussed it as a positive thing, that it was best if they focused on bringing back segregation. In time, they'd also deal with all those immigrants coming in to destroy the white race. Chase wasn't sure he believed any of those things would ever happen, but his family and everyone else around him sure did, including the wealthy people who sometimes gave money to AR.

As the night wore on and continued to get colder and scarier, deep in the back of his mind, was also the worry of that wild boar he'd been after. What if the animal came running through the edge of the woods and fell into the sinkhole with them? He knew it was probably a stupid concern, but still, it was there. Along with the damn rainstorm. For a second he thought about sharing his worry with Larke, but decided against it. The last thing he wanted was for her start acting stupid and get all panicky about something that wasn't going to happen anyway.

But she didn't panic once since we've been down here.

Chase ignored the voice in his head, the one that was trying to make it seem as if he doing something good by not giving her another reason to worry.

"Do you want to hear a story?"

No. He shrugged. "Why ask? You'll still keep talking even if I say no."

He thought he heard her laugh. He wasn't sure. Didn't care. On second thought, maybe her story *would* be a step above listening to the annoying chirping of crickets and all sorts of critters occupying the woods.

"A hedgehog and a firefly lived in the same building. Every single day they saw each other but never ever talked…"

The last thing Chase remembered was the sound of Larke yawning as she finished her childish story. Blinking the sleep from his eyes, he realized they'd both fallen asleep. Also, it wasn't as dark as before. The other thing he noticed was the weight on his shoulder. His first instinct was to push her away, uncaring if she hit her head in the process. But he didn't. Since being trapped down here, somehow it no longer seemed to make much of a difference that he hated or was *supposed* to hate the girl next to him. They had bigger things to worry about.

Like the loud clap of thunder and the fat drops of rain hitting their cold skin, that caused Larke to suddenly wake up screaming. Bolting upright, Chase turned to face her. Their gazes locked and held. Larke's eyes were huge and wide with fear. He wondered if she could see the same in his, despite trying so hard to remain brave.

"It might not last long. Sometimes we get these five minutes rain," he said, unsure if he was trying to make Larke or himself feel better.

It wasn't a five-minute rain shower. A flash of lightning split the early morning sky, in a violent display of might. The clouds ripped open, pelting them with drop after drop of torrential rain. In unison, they both began shouting, frantic screams as they tested their luck of escaping before the water piled in, filling the sinkhole. Not a single sound came back except for the violent downpour pounding the dirt.

Soaking wet, with the rain coursing down their faces, they stared at each other. Larke was crying, her shoulders jerking up and down. "I don't want to die in here, Chase. I want my mom. I just want to be home with my mom."

He wanted to cry too. Chase looked down, wondering how long it would take for the hole to completely fill with water if it was already on his knees. He raised his head, numb and unsure if he was crying or not. His mind became a tangled mess. For some reason, he was thinking about that dead chink reporter again. His death had happened so fast. The man hadn't really…suffered. He and Larke, though… They were so young. And drowning would mean a whole lot of suffering. Painful and slow, he imagined. His heartbeat thumped inside his chest as he inched closer to Larke. Chase stretched out his hand, reaching for hers. She was gazing up at him, her lips trembling as she continued to cry. His eyes burned the moment his fingers brushed lightly against Larke's. He opened his mouth to lie, assure her that drowning happened quickly. He never had the chance.

A booming voice from above called out to them. "Hey, is anyone down there?" A bright light beamed into the hole. Chase jumped away from Larke. Peering down at them was a man with a thick beard, wearing a silver badge.

"Jesus Christ," the man muttered, shaking his head. "Don't worry kids. I'll be back in a second." Behind him, a woman could be heard asking the sheriff if he wanted the rope.

From that point on, everything else happened in a whirlwind. After the sheriff and his officer freed them from the sinkhole, still shivering and dripping wet, Chase watched as Larke, also shivering and soaked, slowly reached around her neck and unclasped her necklace. She held out her trembling hand. "I want you to have this."

He gaped at her, knowing fully well they were being watched. The sheriff knew who he was because moments ago the man had asked him if he was Joseph Butler's grandson.

Chase shook his head. "I don't want it."

"Maybe you will," she insisted. "I go to Heron Glades Elementary School. Miss Allen's fourth-grade class. Keep it and let me know when we can be friends, okay?"

Because he didn't want to embarrass her in front of the sheriff and the policewoman, Chase took the necklace and shoved it into the pocket of his soaking wet jeans. He gave her a fleeting glance as the policewoman helped her into the car. Steeling himself for whatever was to come, Chase turned to the sheriff, pushing Larke from his mind. What she was obviously still too stupid to understand was, the day of 'friendship' she was hoping for would never come. What happened to them—being so close together, along with his decision to reach for her hand in what he'd assume was one of their final moments—was a mistake. An abomination, a word he'd recently learned from his Bible studies. A big one, that he would never, could never let his family find out about. As far as he knew, he'd been trapped inside that sinkhole all by himself.

Chapter One

L arke was on a winning streak. Well, she was *supposed* to be on a winning streak. And it would've been fine, if she didn't have to deal with Kevin her date, finding any and every excuse to put his hands on her. Mainly on her bottom. Still…not even Kevin and his fast hands could kill her happiness.

Agreeing to her friend Riva's suggestion of an evening out bowling had been as much about spending time together as kicking back and celebrating the green light she'd received to continue her successful Little Badger children's book series.

Larke stood, taking note of Riva's boyfriend Jason attempting some sort of super bowling maneuver that he claimed was guaranteed to deliver a strike. When the stunt utterly failed and he ended up flat on his butt, she threw her head back and laughed, even harder as Jason scrambled to get back on his feet while trying to play it off like nothing happened.

"That's funny, Larke?" he asked, playfully scolding her. She grinned and raised her hand, wiping the tears of laughter from her eyes. Larke paused in mid-action, suddenly realizing she was the only one grinning. She became all too aware of the eerie silence that fell across the floor. Puzzled, she noticed Kevin shaking his head in disgust. She followed his gaze and stopped.

Oh. Now she understood. A sliver of dread wedged itself in the pit of her stomach. Standing in front of the clerk's desk was a man. A monster actually, though not in terms of possessing an ugly face. No. This was something else. Something that sickened her and represented so much that was wrong in the world today.

Even worse, his attention was centered on her and her friends. Mostly her. Because she was the darkest? Laughing too loud? Fear skidded across her skin and burrowed deep. And yet…she couldn't help but stare the way rubberneckers did while annoyingly holding up traffic.

Just look away. She couldn't. A bevy of emotions compelled and paralyzed her, leaving her with no choice *but* to look at him. The man was tall, much taller than the clerk who was the same height as her five feet six inches. Dave–the clerk stood and his head barely reached the top of the other man's wide chest.

But it wasn't this guy's height that stood out or the way his body appeared to be carved from solid rock. No, it was the horrible, disgusting tattoos covering the length of his bare arms. On one hand, Larke and just about anyone else who took a close look, could make out the words, 'White Pride' inked vertically and stopping at his wrist. Further down, on the back of that same hand was the Celtic cross, which she recognized as a symbol of racial hatred. It ran all the way down then tapered off into curved lines that laced toward the edge of his knuckles. From what she could see of his other hand, it was also covered in tattoos. No doubt, those were racist symbols too.

Beside her, Riva nervously asked, "Do you think we should leave? I mean the place is closing soon anyway?" Larke could see the trepidation on her friend's features and understood. Riva was originally from India. It was well known that white supremacists weren't big on immigrants. Unless they were well, white, she supposed.

Larke never had the chance to answer her friend. Kevin mumbled his annoyance, "Forget him. We came here to bowl," he whipped his hand in the direction of the desk, "not stand around staring at some fucked up klan-boy." He turned to Larke and grinned, seemingly impressed with his remark then slapped her on the bottom.

This was the third time he'd done so tonight. Fists curled and trying so hard to maintain her composure, Larke gritted her teeth. "I'd like for you to move away from me, Kevin. Because the next time you touch me, I'm not sure if the bowling ball will strike the pins or your head. It could honestly go either way." She stepped away, counting her blessing that she'd driven here alone and not with him.

Her game suffered for the rest of the time. Larke wasn't a big bowler and rarely even went out on dates, but tonight had been going great until her mind became frazzled and dazed. She could no longer focus on the game or enjoy the time away from her apartment.

Her twenty-two-year-old mind was centered on another time and place. A bad place. When she was nine and deep inside the sinkhole with Chase. They'd spent a cold night huddled together beneath the sweater she'd grabbed from her mom's car, because her own clothes were scattered or unpacked after the move. Despite so many years gone by, she had never forgotten that angry white boy or the things he'd told her.

That man could very well be a member of Antebellum Resistance, the hate group Chase's family belonged to. Maybe he even lived around or in Lee's Fortress. She'd been there once, driven through it with her mother some years ago. The town had appeared semi-rundown. Neither Larke nor her mother had wanted to venture farther inside the racist community, despite her fanciful dreams of seeing Chase and recognizing him. Why? She hadn't been sure. Perhaps to see what became of him. To know he'd turned out fine.

Through the corner of her eye, Larke could see the man exiting the building. The room itself seemed to breathe a sigh of relief. Over at the desk, the clerk who earlier appeared to have been on the verge of hyperventilating, issued everyone a tepid smile then pretended to busy himself by shuffling around a stack of paper.

The rest of the evening went by in a bit of a daze. The relaxing night she'd been looking forward to all day long now felt ruined. Tainted. It was hard to concentrate on the conversation around her in between rounds of bowling. She'd even ended up yelling at Kevin again when he'd accidentally touched her. She hated yelling or being angry. Nothing good ever came of it. Larke was known by the few friends she had as being calm, always happy and trying to keep others around her feeling the same.

But after the racist guy left, it became almost impossible to pretend any sort of calm. Her mind refused to let go. Kept going back to the evening she'd stupidly taken the wrong city bus after school because the school bus's route didn't include her area. Her mother's schedule as a nurse had been rearranged for that day so the afternoon before they'd gone over exactly what Larke needed to do to get home. At the time she hadn't thought it a big deal and had been so sure she could handle the short bus ride from the school to her house, where she'd wait at an elderly neighbor's until her mom got home. It all went so wrong.

Larke sighed, shaking herself from the memory of Lee's Fortress. She needed her head on right for the drive home. In the hurry to leave the bowling alley, she made it halfway to her car before realizing she'd forgotten her sweater inside. It was a just in case it's cold sweater. The summer months meant businesses went overboard blasting their air conditioning. A quick run inside and she was able to grab the cardigan from the clerk's desk.

For a second, Larke was tempted to ask the clerk—who, thankfully didn't seem as shaken as he did before—if people like that man frequented the bowling alley. She didn't. First, she didn't want to risk the look of terror she'd seen on his face earlier and second, she had absolutely no plans of returning here. If the white supremacist hadn't been there to bowl like everyone else, she didn't want to begin contemplating what the other reasons could be.

Larke made it back outside to the lit parking lot. In spite of being alone, she was relieved to see Kevin had driven off. That had been a disaster, she mused while hurrying to her car. She had almost made it when a figure emerged from behind the corner of the building. Larke froze in her steps. Fear thundered through her. It was the same man from earlier. The white supremacist. Her knees almost buckled as he edged closer to the car and stopped there. Right beside the driver's side door.

Nerves and adrenaline pumped through her blood, making her nauseous with it. She'd been so close to going home. So close and tonight should've been wonderful, not end with her facing down a monster.

Why me? Apart from the obvious. Honestly, why her?

Instincts kicking in, Larke unzipped her handbag and whipped out her phone. She took a careful step backward, then another, all the while contemplating the best exit strategy to safety. Her gaze flashed to the window of the bowling alley. They were closing early tonight and had already started cleaning up when she'd gone inside to retrieve her sweater. Was the door locked? If so, surely they'd open it in response to her frantic banging. She hoped. Prayed.

Her heart slammed against her ribcage. The man was staring at her as if he had all night to stand and watch her squirm. She tightened her grip around the phone inside her now sweating palm. He stepped forward and her mouth went bone dry. His voice, when he finally spoke, was low and rough, a deep timbre. "Put the phone away."

Her fingers tightened like steel clamps around the plastic casing. No way. She was no fool. Still, Larke didn't trust herself to speak or move. Would he kidnap her? Rape her? They both knew if she were to dial for help, it would never arrive fast enough before he was able to subdue her.

"I–I have money inside my bag," she said shakily, already dipping a hand into her bag, fishing for her wallet. The sound of her erratic breathing and the pounding of her heart rattled her eardrums.

"Don't want your money," he answered. His blue eyes appeared cold and unrelenting beneath the glare of the light. "Not what I came here for."

Her fingers stilled around the wallet at the note of mockery she detected. Her fear amused him.

He's going to toy with me and then kill me.

Larke managed a weak nod. She then shot a furtive glance over her shoulder, making a mental note of the faint light inside the bowling alley. Someone might still be in there. If she made a run for it…

Preparing to do just that, she drew in a muted breath and held it in as her tormentor opened his mouth. His relaxed demeanor showed her the pleasure he took in knowing she had no choice but to stay put and listen to him, and the words he uttered next, confirmed what he truly was.

"That nigger you were standing next to in there." He jerked his head toward the bowling alley. "You screwing him?"

Her mind went blank. It had been one thing knowing he was a white supremacist based on his tattoos, but to hear those actual hateful words. Her head and heart began to ache all at once. How was she supposed to react to this? If she lashed out or tried to lecture, surely it would send him into a rage with her being on the receiving end.

Larke swallowed hard, forcing air into her lungs. A thought struck her. Maybe she was simply caught up in something Kevin did. If so, she wanted no part of it. "If this is about Kevin, you need to know we're only friends. If even. We had a few classes together at the community college, but that's all. I really don't know much else about him, if you thought I had information to give you."

A muscle in his jaw ticked. "You didn't answer my question. Are you fucking him? Yes or no?"

Larke gaped, nearly stumbling on her shock. Was he serious?

He was staring at her intently. So apparently, he was. She shook her head. "No."

He relaxed his stance, seemingly satisfied with her answer. Larke bit the inside of her cheek, silently praying he'd leave now and allow her access to her car. The man held firm, not budging an inch. He scraped a long finger against his square jaw, scratching in a distracted manner while holding her hostage within his sight.

Against her better judgment, Larke took the time to study his appearance. Despite his terrifying demeanor, he looked young. His eyes were a deep shade of blue and his light brown hair was cut short but not buzz cut low. If she had to guess his age, she'd peg him to be in his mid-twenties. Not much older than herself.

Once again, Larke cast a furtive glance at the bowling alley. Her heart sank at the unexpected darkness. All the lights were now off. Taking a chance, that maybe just maybe, this guy had gotten whatever information he'd wanted from her, she asked nicely. "Can I get to my car, please? My parents are waiting for me. If I don't get home soon, they'll start to worry and come searching for me." God, how she wished her mom *was* actually alive and waiting for her.

"Your father's waiting for you too?"

Larke grimaced. Of all the questions... She tried not to flinch and continued staring at him, wondering if he'd recognized her for the awful liar she was. Taking a deep breath, she doubled down. "Yes, my father too."

His lips curled into a smirk. "I thought he lived in Missouri."

In that moment, her heart skidded to the center of her throat. She squinted her eyes. *What?* That single word was the only thought her mind could frame because impossible as it was, time itself no longer mattered. Felt as if it had been erased.

Larke stared at the man in front of her. She pushed her fear from earlier to a far recess of her mind then allowed herself time. Time to survey this racist who had cornered her outside the parking lot of a fucking bowling alley. She searched his eyes and his features.

She analyzed even his voice, hearing him inside her head in a way she'd never thought to before.

Not much older than myself.

She heard her younger self talking, trying to figure out the boy who refused to acknowledge her presence beside him. *"Why do you have that knife? You're just a kid. Not much older than myself. I bet you took it from your daddy and he doesn't know."*

Feeling like a first-class idiot, she dared to ask a question for which she already knew the answer. "How do you know where my dad lives?"

Awaiting his reply, Larke scoured her gaze on him. This couldn't be Chase. It couldn't be him, her mind screamed. The tattoos... Placed right there on his arms for the world to see his hate and true colors. *Please let this be a joke. A mistake.* She didn't want this sick individual who had used an evil slur to describe Kevin and had outright demanded to know about her sex life, to be the boy she knew. This was not how Chase was supposed to be. Not the way she'd imagined him.

Over the years, he should've realized racism was wrong. Maybe even talked to his family about it and... And nothing. Larke shook her head, feeling foolish, disappointed and heartbroken. No wonder he'd never tried to contact her. He hated her for the one thing she'd had no control over. Her race.

Seconds ticked by without an answer from *Chase.* It didn't bother her. His answer no longer mattered. She loosened her fingers around the phone, vaguely aware of it slipping and falling into her bag.

"You're not gonna try and run?" He eyed her with suspicion.

Larke shook her head weakly. "No." *She* felt weak. Shell-shocked. "I haven't forgotten what happened the last time I ran from you. It didn't do either of us any good."

"Sure didn't," he muttered, his gaze resting on her face.

Larke rummaged through her mind for something to say. She

was leery and uncertain of where all of this was headed seeing as he'd yet to make a threatening move toward her. She surveyed his hands, which were empty and asked with a hint of sarcasm that was meant to garner a reaction, anything to reveal his intentions. "Did you leave your knife at home this time?"

His lips slanted into a taunting smile. "I think I can handle you without one."

Larke sighed. Everything about him felt like a slap in the face. This wasn't how it should be. *You were supposed to have been my friend,* Larke silently yelled. How sad that she was now standing here wondering if he would ultimately harm her once he grew tired of their banter.

"Chase." Saying his name felt like an oddity to her tongue, as if he didn't even deserve to have her acknowledge him with a name. "*Is* there anything for us to talk about?" She held out her hands, palms up. "In case you haven't noticed I'm still black. When you insulted Kevin a while ago, you also insulted me."

She stood there, patiently awaiting his answer. His attention shifted to across the parking lot and Larke followed, both watching as Dave the clerk spotted them and began scurrying to his car on the opposite end. He was pretending not to have seen them. Her, a black female being harassed by the white supremacist he'd spoken to earlier. Again, her stomach twisted. Didn't he care that she might need help?

All thoughts of the clerk's callous disregard for her safety fled when Chase finally spoke. "No. There's not really anything for us to talk about."

"Then why are you bothering with me?"

His gaze skimmed over her frame. Larke folded her arms across her middle, feeling more uncomfortable than before. His eyes held hers, glinting with... Larke frowned. She was unable to discern what the look meant, because within a split second, a mask of utter disinterest shadowed his features. "Maybe I'm bored," he murmured. "Maybe I don't have nothing better to do tonight than stand out here talking to you."

"You're not going to do anything to me?" she asked, peering up at him.

No answer. Annoyed Larke shook her head and took a tentative step forward. "Fine. Since there's nothing left to say, can I please get to my car? It's getting late, I'm tired and I just want to go home."

The smug grin returned. "Soon. I'll let you go real soon."

Right then and there, she knew he was playing a cat and mouse game with her. He still hadn't answered her question, if he intended to harm her or not.

She clasped her hands together and plastered a sugary smile to her lips. "Okay, Chase. I'm all ears. What do you want to talk about?"

"Not like that," he grated. His jaws hardened. "I'm not dumb. I know when someone is fucking with me. Don't do that."

"What do you expect me to say? I don't know you. I'm surprised you recognized me after all these years. I didn't recognize you. As far as I can tell, you hate me and because of that, you're keeping me from leaving. What else do you expect me to say?"

His brows narrowed. He surveyed her up and down, then drew his head up, locking his darkened gaze on hers. "You look different now, Larke. Grew into your fatness."

"Um yeah." She blinked. *None of this is real.* "You uh… you look different too." A lot different. She slid her focus to his arms. From here, she could see the tattoos on his other arm were also hate related. Her heart sank lower and lower. Raising her head, Larke caught Chase watching her. He growled, "They ain't going away so get that fucking look off your face."

She sucked in a tremulous breath. "You're not making this very easy. This whole talking thing."

"Are you still writing stories?" He blurted the question out of the blue, anger gone as he switched the subject entirely.

Larke parted her lips; shocked that he remembered. "Yeah," she answered slowly. "I still write." Pride grabbed a hold and got the best her. "I have three books in the bookstores. I write for children. No surprise."

Chase recalling her being a fat little girl stuffing her face with sugar was one thing, but this; such a minute detail about her. That was…unexpected. Still, the revelation changed nothing. Chase was *not* a good person.

He nodded yet remained silent, simply watching her, which prompted Larke to ask, "Did you really wait out here for me because you had nothing better to do?"

He lifted a shoulder. "Why else? I don't kill time by harassing women if that's what you're thinking."

Fair enough. "I'm confused because, despite our past, I'm not exactly the type of person you normally *mingle* with." Her brows knitted. "I'm honestly trying to make sense out of us standing around talking when it's pretty obvious this shouldn't be happening."

He chuckled low. "Don't worry. This was a one-off. I don't make a habit of talking to nig—"

"Don't," Larke whispered, holding up a hand, warding him off. "Don't ever call me that." Angered and hurt, she drew herself up, no longer able to keep her silence. "You used that word before and I was too afraid to speak up when I should have."

"And you're not scared now?" he challenged. Still, he made no move toward her. She squeezed her eyes shut, swallowed down the nerves that caused her heart to beat rapidly inside her chest then reopened them. It was obvious Chase knew she, like any sane person, was terrified of him. Knew and relished it, she imagined. As she had done earlier, Larke slipped a hand inside her bag, curling her fingers around the phone like a lifeline.

She stood straight and raised her chin. "I'm going to ask you one more time to please move away from my car. I want to go home, Chase. I'm exhausted and you've ruined my evening."

"I ruined your evening by talking to you?"

He had the audacity to sound shocked. Was staring at her with his brows arched as if *she* had offended him.

Larke stiffened. "Not by talking to me. You've ruined my evening by using that horrible word twice in front of me. The messing with my head I could tolerate, but not the slurs. If you try to stop me from reaching my car I'll call for help. It doesn't matter if no one helps me right away. At least it'll be on record that I called. The clerk also saw me with you last. There are probably cameras around here too."

"I get your point," he said flatly. "It's cool." He held up his hands while backing away. His movements were exaggerated and telling. Her threat much like her fear, amused him.

Reaching for her keys, Larke took one hesitant step after the other as Chase continued moving further back until there was a safe distance between him, her and the car. She breathed a heavy sigh of relief the minute she was seated behind the wheel with the engine on and doors locked. Eyeing him one last time, Larke carefully exited the parking lot, forcing herself to not waste another second looking back on Chase.

Chapter Two

There were a few things that Chase was certain of in life. The first being, he was a proud racist and would tell this to anyone without blinking an eye. The second was, at some point he would take over the group his grandfather had started. Antebellum Resistance was becoming one of the biggest neo-Confederate nationalist groups in North Carolina and hopefully in the entire country one day. The second one was merely a forecast for his future. At twenty-four he was still young and had other things to occupy him. Plus, it wasn't as if his stepfather Trevor planned on stepping down as leader any time soon.

That first certainty in his life, though… That one had Chase's mind in a twist tonight. More messed up than his mind had been when he'd agreed to collect membership dues from the paranoid owner of the bowling alley, who was in constant fear of someone finding out about the people he associated with. Anyone, except for the idiot clerk who they all knew was too terrified to say anything.

He'd entered the building feeling like a damn fool for playing pick up boy tonight and left feeling worse than a fool. Like a traitor. The worst kind he knew–a race traitor. He'd walked out the door of the bowling alley stunned and in disbelief after realizing the woman, whose throaty and bubbly laughter had caused his brain to blank and made him turn around and stare; was everything he *hadn't* expected or liked.

Barely able to listen to the stuttering clerk's attempt at finding the envelope, Chase had stopped altogether after hearing the sound of a girl laughing. When he'd turned around to see the face and body it belonged to, his stomach had plummeted with disappointment. All he could see was a black girl with long dark braids and her mouth opened. The laughter had died on her thick lips as her dark almond-shaped eyes focused on him, widening like a deer right before his hunting bullet pierced the neck. Come to think of it, she'd looked like that the entire time after he'd cornered her in the parking lot.

Despite her race and his traitorous thoughts, Chase had somehow managed to convince himself it was important to heed the ache in his balls and the twitching of cock that happened the moment he allowed his eyes to wash over her curvy figure, clad in a tight pair of cut-off jeans that hugged her waist and clung to her plump, round ass. His mouth went dry recalling the outline of her large breasts under the silky v-neck shirt she wore. Faced with his body's immediate reaction to her, he'd still waited for the disgust that was bound to come, simply for allowing himself to give a creature like that a second glance.

When the disgust failed to appear, Chase's mind went into overdrive imagining what her body looked like under those clothes. Before he'd even heard her name and put two and two together, that this was the same chubby girl he'd nearly died with, he was already formulating a plan to get her alone. Luck was on his side when she'd left her friends and went back into the bowling alley for her sweater.

Chase hoped once he had her alone and got a real good look at her, talked to her after all these years, that he'd come across a flaw–apart from the obvious–that would really churn his warped stomach.

Still waiting.

The moment never came. Larke had no flaws. At least none that he could visibly see—which in a way made him feel pissed but relieved at the same time because he *liked* being aroused for her. Blood pumped through his veins and rushed to his cock, giving him a steel hard erection. It felt so fucking good, unlike anything he'd ever felt before. And that was why he was seated inside his pickup, waiting outside Larke's apartment building.

Deep inside Chase knew what he was doing was wrong. Hell, he wasn't even sure what he planned to do now that he knew her address. Tonight was the first time he'd trailed a girl home. He was no stalker, had never considered or found the need to do anything like this before. Something about her was screwing with his head and it needed to end. Fast.

A light went on inside an apartment on the second floor. That had to be her place, he thought, shoving down another bout of conscience. He wasn't doing anything wrong. He lived in a free country. If he wanted to sit in his truck outside some darkie girl's apartment, he could. And if his dick was getting excited again thinking about her, well there was nothing he could do to stop it.

Right?

Earlier, he'd led Larke to believe boredom was his main reason for waylaying her in the parking lot, but in all honesty, the idea wasn't that hard to believe. What if it *was* just a matter of boredom causing wild irrational thoughts to rampage through his head? It wasn't that far-fetched that he might be bored from always sleeping with the same type of females. Chase tapped a finger to the steering wheel, picturing the last couple of girls he'd fucked. Hmm. They'd all been slender and thin, much thinner than Larke, who made him think of softness and lush flesh that a man could hold on to while he… No! He shook his head, refusing to allow his thoughts to run *that* far off course.

Body type aside, Chase knew it had nothing to do with his previous one-nighters being alike. It couldn't because he was only attracted to white girls. At the first sight of Larke tonight, his dick should've fallen right back to sleep instead of standing at full mast in hopes of getting her attention. If he really was in the market for a change–someone 'exotic'–then wouldn't he have been better off scoping out a female spic? One with enough European blood to overshadow whatever else they were usually mixed with. An Asian chick would also be the better choice than sitting here like a perv alone in his pickup, his mind and body raging for a black chick he barely knew.

I'm going to hell.

Seriously. If he believed hell existed like his mother described during the Bible lessons she'd given him–before she'd run off while he was stuck in the sinkhole–Chase knew he more than likely had a room of torture awaiting him. A real special one for idiots like him.

Grunting his frustration, he gave a fleeting glance toward Larke's apartment then drove away. He was unsure about his next move *if* there'd be a next move, all things considered. Like her being terrified of him. Chase frowned as his conscience took another unexpected hit. At first, he'd found it amusing, watching Larke squirm while blocking the entrance to her driver's side door.

Messing with her hadn't been as fulfilling as it should've been, Chase decided. He kept picturing the way her eyes, filled with fear stared at the tattoos on his arms. He'd yelled at her about it too, hadn't he?

"Probably shouldn't have done that," he muttered to himself.

His phone vibrated a second before the trill ringing jarred his thoughts from Larke. Chase welcomed the interruption until he saw the name that popped up on the display. It was Haley, a slim brunette with real pretty green eyes and just enough curves to escape being called boyish. She was also one of the latest girls his stepfather tried to push him onto. Or rather them onto him. Haley had also grown up in the same community as him.

The phone continued to ring, but Chase ignored it. When it finally stopped, he eyed the display with a pang of regret as the light faded. He should've answered. If she was calling after nine in the night, he doubted it was his voice she was wanting to hear. Which was fine by him. Haley was the exact medicine he needed to get rid of the traitorous thoughts inside his head and ease the pressure in his balls.

Good thing too, because her place was on the way to his house. The drive from Larke's apartment to Lee's Fortress took about thirty minutes. The small township begun by his grandfather was on the outskirt of a larger city and was once occupied by coal miners before the mines were shut out of business. There was nothing charming or nice about the town. The houses, even the newer ones built years ago when AR first started up, were a paint's peel away from appearing run-down. But for the people who lived and grew up here, it was the only place they were guaranteed interaction with those who looked like them and shared the same beliefs and concerns.

Speaking of… He let out a groan and shook his head at the sight of Trevor standing outside the house Chase had lived in as a kid. Smoke wafted around his stepfather as the older man waved a hand in the air, flagging him down.

Shit. Trevor was the last person he wanted to see or talk to tonight. Because he had no other choice, Chase slowed his truck to a halt. He retrieved the envelope he'd received from the clerk, then walked toward the man who'd helped to raise him. As much as he'd wanted to keep going, pretending he hadn't seen the slim man with his hair drawn back into a ponytail, Chase knew if Trevor stopped him on his way home, this wasn't for any stepfather-son talk. He followed behind the leader of Antebellum Resistance, taking a seat across from him on the porch.

"Took your ass long enough to get back," Trevor drawled, kicking one leg across a small table scattered with ashes and cigarette butts.

Chase shrugged and dropped the envelope on the table, not the least bit offended by his stepfather's words. Trevor spoke like that to everyone. Even Louise, Chase's mother, and Trevor's ex-wife. Chase hadn't done that. He'd always spoken to his mom with respect.

Didn't stop her one bit from dropping him like hot coal, pushing him completely out of her life.

"You were waiting out here for me all this time?" he asked Trevor, who was reaching into his shirt pocket for a cigarette.

Trevor nodded then leaned his head to the side, his entire body jerking up and down from coughing. Chase looked on with a mixture of disgust and fascination. No matter how often he'd witness Trevor's hacking cough over the years, the man never failed to keep lighting up and puffing away.

"You want me to get you some water? Medicine?"

Trevor flicked his hand in the air. "I'm good, man. Got a doctor's appointment coming up soon. Hope he can give me something to get this shit under control."

New pair of lungs? Chase nodded, humoring the man. "Lots of new medicine out there."

"Hmm," Trevor said absently. He drew himself up in the chair, scratching his chin. "You still planning that trip down to Jacksonville next Friday?"

"I have to. This is the only chance I have to talk with that new captain I hired before the ship sails." Chase was the sole owner of a cargo ship. He'd bought the old ship two years ago with his grandfather. They'd purchased it after meeting up with an old family friend who was tired of the industry and desperately wanted the ship off his hands. Chase had plans of turning that one ship into a successful cargo fleet sometime in the future.

Trevor knew this. Knew Chase wanted to keep everything legal without any authorities breathing down his neck for something he'd worked so hard for. But in the end, it would make no difference. He'd have to do what was best for the group. Antebellum Resistance was his legacy. He'd *always* have to do right by the group and their struggle before himself. Staring at his stepfather and knowing what was about to come, Chase silently counted down the seconds, waiting for the order that would be wrapped inside a request.

Another puff on the cigarette. A fit of coughing and the countdown ended. "I got a friend who works near the port. Got himself an exporting company. Lots of connections with foreign ships and customs."

"Trevor. Honest to God, I don't have time for any stories. I told you last time that my shipping business is completely separate from AR."

"I know. And I'm telling you I wouldn't ask if it wasn't real important. I was trying not to say anything but since you're dragging this out. Money's running tight these days and some of our sponsors are getting stingy. Too many pussies out there scared of showing their pride." A swirl of smoke rose from the edge of his mouth and drifted in the air. "You remember what that was like, don't you? We got lots of kids here. Lots of em."

Hungry children. Chase ground his teeth, holding tight to his anger. He got the damn point. Trevor didn't need to drive it in. "How much money are we talking about?"

"Fifty grand. More or less. We can handle it just like last time. Use the same people."

"Yeah, okay. Since you have it all planned out. All I wanna know is what the hell are we talking about this time? Old ass DVDs? Food? Bootleg crap? I'm lost here. Last time I let you do this, I said I didn't wanna know what all that shit was, but fuck… Seriously, man. What is it this time?"

"Like I was telling you. This friend of mine took a trip over to Singapore the other day. Business." Trevor rolled his eyes. "Trust me, he didn't wanna go."

Chase let out a loud breath. "No stories. Just say it. What exactly are *we* sending over there?"

Trevor chuckled. "You ain't gotta look like that, man. It's only liquor."

"Liquor?"

"Nothing more, nothing less. Good ol' American booze," he said, holding his hands out wide.

Chase scowled. "You want to smuggle booze into Singapore. Let me guess–to dealers who'll jack up the price for chinks who wanna get drunk?"

Trevor straightened his shoulders and snapped his fingers together. "Bout sums it up. You catch on quickly, boy. If that no-good mother of yours had stuck around, can't say she wouldn't have been proud of you."

Chase snorted. He knew for a fact Louise wouldn't have felt pride or anything for him. He wondered if Trevor even believed the crap that came out of his mouth. Luckily, Chase knew him well enough to see his smooth talk for what it was. Buttering up. Something his stepfather never had to do when Chase was a kid and had to follow instructions or feel the belt.

"Trevor," Chase began, "you know I'm dedicated to everything my grandfather started. To everything we have and want to happen. But that doesn't mean I want us to live with the Feds being more suspicious than they already are. I'm just saying, don't make this a habit. I know you're in charge and everything. I'm good with that. I respect everything you've done. But you gotta remember that everyone's got a limit at some point."

Trevor nodded while puffing away on his cigarette. "Gotcha. No hard feelings. I know you busted your ass working in Deek's hunting store, taking all them crazy hours to save up enough money so Joe could see you were serious about buying that old ship with him.

Chase rose from his chair, pinning Trevor with a measured stare. "Then you know exactly what I mean when I say this is the last time."

Trevor held up his hands. "As long as you get your ass down to Jacksonville, we're good. I'll give you the info later. You can take Jesse McNair with you. He can transport the liquor."

Soon after leaving Trevor's place, Chase forced himself to push his stepfather and his shady dealings from his mind. It wasn't until an hour later as he climbed into bed that he remembered his plan to stop by Haley's house and see what she had to offer. Chase groaned inside his head, knowing that idea wouldn't have made one lick of a difference. He wouldn't have gone through with seeing Haley because all he could focus on was Larke. Her dark eyes wide with fear and confusion, staring at the words and symbols on his arms.

He turned over in bed, angry that he was *still* thinking about her. Larke's opinion meant nothing to him. *She* was nothing. He didn't give one fuck what she thought about him. In fact, tomorrow he was going to pay Haley a visit and ride her so damn hard until a certain part of his body remembered exactly where its loyalty rested.

Chapter Three

Putting pen to paper, or rather finding the right words to tap on the keyboard was difficult today. It hadn't been before. Not this hard. Sadly, Larke knew the reason why. Ever since last week, her mind refused to stay in one place. Almost every time she closed her eyes, she'd find herself back inside the woodlands in Lee's Fortress. She wound her arms around her middle. The very name of the town made her shudder.

Sick.

Just like Chase's treatment of her the other night. Over the years, she'd made up numerous scenarios of seeing him again. But not once had any of them played out like it did outside the bowling alley. The cold reality of what and who a grown-up Chase had become kept her awake some nights.

Larke closed her laptop. She would get no writing done today. Not for the first time this year, she wished her mother was still alive. Maggie Taylor had been a trusted friend, the only person Larke would've been able to confide her true feelings to. To let her know how much it bothered her even now, thinking about Chase, knowing he would sooner hurt her than be her friend. Not that she needed him as a friend. Simply, what if…

People have to choose their own destiny, Larke. You can't force someone to believe the same things you do. All you can do is hear them out and if you're determined to change their mind you have to understand it won't happen by force or arguing. Maggie had flashed her a smile and ruffled her hair. *You'll learn more when you get older, baby.*

Those gems of wisdom from her mother were said so many years ago when Larke had broken down one day, months after the incident and confessed all the awful things Chase had told her about the people he lived with. That he too seemed to believe the same horrible things about people like her and her mother.

All the logic in the world couldn't erase the sting. Chase had *chosen* his destiny. In spite of what he'd been taught, he was a grown man and at some point, there should've been an eye opener that racism was wrong. Evil. No one could remain a white supremacist unless they chose to be. And he'd chosen that path.

Letting out a loud breath, Larke shook her head. Pondering a man like Chase did not go hand in hand with writing innocent children's stories. She crossed her arms behind her head and stretched out across the blanket she'd laid on the grass. The sun shone bright and the July temperature was more akin to mid-day than early morning. The park was quiet, despite the numerous people walking their dogs, or going for a morning jog. In another hour or two, the area would get livelier and it would be much harder for her to concentrate.

She closed her eyes, determined to bring the scenery inside her head onto the blank page awaiting her words. Little rabbit flitting across a field. Lots of sunshine and…a shadow. A shadow was over the rabbit? Larke's eyes flew open. She blinked. This was reality. There was no rabbit. But there definitely was something blocking her sunlight. Correction. Someone.

Larke bolted upright, her mouth went dry as dust at the sight of Chase standing at the foot of her blanket, dressed in a pair of jeans and a long-sleeved shirt.

The frantic beating of her heart and the remnants of fear caused Larke to do a quick survey of the grassy area, checking to make sure there were still people milling about. Relieved that there were others to witness their interaction, she drew in a deep breath and willed her nerves to calm.

"Good morning," she said, hoping her casual tone would mask the sliver of dread that refused to leave.

He nodded, offering no greeting in return. Surprisingly, he lowered himself, sitting at the edge of her blanket as if she'd issued an invitation. He rounded his gaze on her. "You still afraid of me?"

"I…"

"You are," he interrupted flatly. "You shouldn't be. I'm not gonna hurt you. I wasn't planning to in the parking lot either. So I don't know why you're acting all scared. I didn't even put my hands on you."

Larke wanted to scream, ask him if he'd conveniently forgotten having chased her with his hunting knife. That she knew what he was capable of. She drew herself up, gaping at him. "Chase, this isn't an act. I watch the news. I have the internet. I'm not naïve. There are too many things about you that tell me I should be afraid. Not only me. People who look like me—those you don't like. Did you know my mother and I were advised by the police lady who brought me home, that it was best not to let anyone know where I'd been? That we were together." She stared at him, her eyes peering into his. "She was a police officer and I could hear the concern and worry in her voice. That's something that stayed with me ever since."

"Did she tell you why?"

"No. Just that it was for the best. I figured it out by myself some time later. Reading up stuff." She let out a sigh. "And now you've become one of the people I should've feared finding me that night. Life is funny, right?"

"Life is surviving." He pushed to his feet. "That's all. Ain't nothing funny about it."

"Is that what you're doing? What you've been doing? Was it survival mode that made you embrace hate?"

Maybe she shouldn't have been so bold, Larke decided seconds later as he stared at her, his entire body taut, bearing down on her. She flinched, watching his eyes grow cold, frostier than his voice when he bit out. "You need to back the fuck up and remember who you're talking to. Yeah, it's nice and cozy for you to sit on your goddamn picnic blanket, acting like some know it all bitch. Judging me and my—"

"I'm not listening," Larke interrupted, standing quickly. "We're done here." She grabbed her bag and laptop, brushing past him.

His hand shot out, jerking her by the elbow. "We're done when I say we're done."

"Yet I shouldn't be afraid of you," she said, her gaze flashing from his hand on her arm to his face.

Chase dropped his hand to his side. "All right," he muttered. The anger evaporated from his tone. "Listen, just relax. I didn't come out here to argue or start anything with you."

Didn't come. Meaning he'd purposely sought her out. As if this could have been a coincidence anyway. Emboldened by the obvious regret on his face, Larke studied him in utter confusion.

"How did you know I'd be here?"

He tilted his head to the side, avoiding her eyes.

So now he's afraid to talk. Larke sighed. "Come on Chase. I need an answer. What is this? It's all so weird. At least for me, it is. I'm guessing it has to be for you too. I just want to know the real reason you waited around for me last week and why you're here now?"

He shoved a hand through his low-cut hair and let out a ragged breath, filled with frustration. So deep, it overshadowed her own.

"I don't know. I swear to God, I don't know. I mean when I first saw you, I didn't recognize you at first. It was basically you, this girl standing there, that I couldn't take my eyes off." He squeezed his eyes as if it pained him to tell her these things. "I didn't want to look at you, okay. You understand that. The things I was thinking, none of that should've been inside my head. When I realized who you were—heard your name and connected the dots. I don't know… I just knew I wasn't gonna leave until I talked to you. Had no idea what the hell I was gonna say, but I couldn't let you leave like that, even if I was wondering if you belonged to that guy."

"First I don't belong to anyone and never will. Second…" Second, she didn't really know. There were too many questions. Most important, was Chase trying to say he was attracted to her? Needed her help, somehow? Larke drew in a deep breath, choosing to use her words carefully.

"Second, did you follow me here?"

"I did."

Okay. Larke pursed her lips, surprised she wasn't freaking out. "Do you also know where I live?"

He said nothing, giving a single nod as confirmation. His gaze held hers. Gauging her reaction.

They stood in silence. Perhaps he was studying her, the same way she did him. Drawing his own conclusions, similar to the ones forming inside her mind right now. Whatever Chase was, she didn't believe him to be a liar. And chances were, he truly meant no harm. If he had, wouldn't he have taken his chance when they were alone?

Before she could change her mind, Larke turned to him and said, "Let's go somewhere else." People were beginning to stare. She reached for the blanket but Chase beat her to it. "I got it," he said, picking up the cloth and folding it.

"So, is this your workplace? Where you come to write?"

"Kind of." She fell into step beside him. "I use to come here while waiting for my shift at O'Malley General Hospital to start. I'd get some pretty good writing in, enough that I was able to write a book that wasn't bad." She pinned him with a sardonic smile, recalling his annoyance when she'd asked to tell him a story. "And apparently other people seemed to like it because now I get paid to write."

Chase shrugged, although she caught the faintest hint of a smile on his firm lips. "What do you do at the hospital?"

"Used to," she said, rounding a corner with him beside her. "I got my two-year RN degree after high school and worked at the hospital like my mother did. I started working part-time at the end of last year and was able to quit a couple of months ago. If I budget right, I can do fine with the royalties I get from my books."

Wow. She had given Chase a mouthful. Larke immediately regretted telling him so much about herself. Had to be because of how little she went out with the opposite sex. Something she would definitely remedy if it prevented her from running her mouth to a white supremacist. One, who also assumed he was entitled to her respect for the simple fact of being who he was.

"I guess your mom must be real proud, huh?"

Her heart felt heavy. "She was," Larke told him, unable to keep out the sadness. "She died over a year ago."

"Oh. Sorry."

"Thanks," she said, glancing over at him carrying the picnic blanket. "My mom was ill for a while." Larke lifted a shoulder. "Life has to go on, right?"

He nodded. "That's true. My grandfather died a year ago too. But like you said—have to keep it moving."

She said nothing to that, only cringing inwardly at exactly what she assumed he had to keep moving. Once they arrived near a large pond, away from the walking trail, Larke stopped and place her laptop bag on a bench. Although the area was empty save for her and Chase, it didn't bother her. Her skin no longer prickled with fear at the thought of being alone with him. In the place of her unease from earlier, was uncertain curiosity.

"Aren't you concerned someone you know might see us out here at some point?" she asked, sitting beside him on the bench.

He shook his head. "No. As for the people I know, most of them wouldn't come around these parts. Too many..." His voice trailed. He averted his gaze as if he'd caught himself before saying something he knew would start an argument. "It's too diverse for the people I know. Not everyone can handle going out in a world that isn't the way we'd like it to be."

Larke stiffened. "How exactly would you like it to be?"

He refused to answer. Issuing her a pointed stare, he grated, "I didn't drive all the way out here to talk race with you, Larke."

Okay. Now they were getting somewhere. "Then why *did* you come? Please tell me. Why did you drive all the way out here from your Aryan homeland to see me, when all we have in common is that we were two kids stuck in a bad situation together? We're nothing to each other. We weren't even friends." *Although I gave you my necklace to keep and remember me by.*

"I wanted to see you."

Those were his only words. Larke waited for him to elaborate, say something else. Nothing. His blue eyes pleaded with her to understand. His gaze, so intense, stroked her face, leaving no misunderstanding. Chase wanted her, despite everything he believed in. She wrapped her arms around her middle. Her entire body shivered with emotions that excited and terrified her.

Complete madness.

Trapped beneath his stare, Larke forced herself to look away. Not for the first time since meeting Chase, she felt the urge to run. To get as far away from him as she could, without a glance backward. But what good would it do? The last time she ran from him, she'd found herself in a different sort of danger. Now, as a grown woman, in spite of everything Chase stood for, there was a faint stirring of butterflies awakening inside her stomach whenever their gazes met. Larke groaned silently. Lord help her, she wasn't even sure she *wanted* to run.

"How can you want to see me when we both know this isn't

right?" She tapped a finger to her chest. "*I'm* not supposed to be right. Not enough for you to have an interest in; apart from wishing me gone." Larke narrowed her eyes and shook her head. She might not want to run from him, but she could still put an end to this insanity. "Whatever this is, I can't. I honestly can't."

Her emotions ran the gamut. Guilt, frustration, anger at herself for actually contemplating allowing Chase into her life, made Larke dizzy with confusion. His jaws hardened as she took the blanket from him. "You understand and agree with me, don't you?" *Please say you do and make this easy.*

Instead of answering, he reached into his back pocket, withdrawing something that at first appeared white and shiny. Larke sucked in a breath as he held out his hand, allowing the pearl necklace to dangle below his finger.

"You kept it?" She opened her mouth, flabbergasted that the plastic pearls were as she'd remembered them. She'd assumed he'd thrown away her friendship gift.

"I planned on throwing it away after you gave it to me," he said, "could never bring myself to go through with it, though. I kept it in a box at the back of my closet. I actually forgot about it for a couple of years until I saw you again."

"Did you clean it," she asked jokingly, trying to wrap her mind around this. "It looks a lot better than when I had it."

His lips twitched into another half-smile. "I wiped it off last night. Didn't think you'd be too impressed if I showed up with your necklace looking grungy."

The smile fell from her lips. "You've known for a while that I come here in the mornings, haven't you?" she asked gently without suspicion. "Were you watching me all the time, at my apartment too?"

"No." A faint tinge of red stained the top of his cheeks. He backtracked. "I mean, okay. I did go back to your apartment building one morning. That's when I followed you here. I never went back to your place. That I swear. I ain't no stalker. I was only trying to figure out the best way to talk to you. That's all. Like I said—it was never about trying to hurt you or anything."

"Then why'd you wait this long to talk to me again?"

He shrugged a lean shoulder. "Because I'm stubborn. I didn't wanna admit that the reason I haven't been able to touch another female is because a black girl who's afraid of me, got my mind all messed up and had me thinking about her all day long."

Larke's mind ceased functioning. She almost wished she could un-hear everything he'd just said. If she could, then she wouldn't have to deal with her heart thumping wildly inside her chest or those ridiculous butterflies in her stomach fully awake and fluttering about like…complete madness. Her lower belly wouldn't cinch with excitement at the idea of Chase constantly thinking about her.

Had he done so at nights too? The brazen question popped into her head before she could reel it in. But reel it in she would. Because as much as her body tingled and felt on the cusp of something…life altering, she still wished she hadn't heard his words. They hurt. She was someone he hadn't asked for or really wanted. His attraction to her was something he was being forced to endure. Feelings she had unintentionally provoked in him. Her. The black girl.

Chapter Four

S omehow, he'd managed to screw up his meeting with Larke. Observing the emotions playing across her face, Chase searched his mind, determined to figure out where it'd started going downhill and ended with her looking so sad. At a complete lost, he remembered the necklace inside his hand.

"How comes you're not asking for your pearls back?"

She gave him a weak smile that somehow made him feel worse. "The necklace by itself isn't important. I gave it to you. Keep it."

Chase groaned inwardly. He quietly waited for her to start telling him off for whatever it was he'd said to upset her this time. Larke did nothing. She wouldn't even make eye contact with him. Her gaze was centered on the damn ducks waddling around beside the pond.

"All right," he grunted. "What'd I say that—"

She turned to him, cutting him off by releasing a loud deep sigh. "I'm Larke. I'm not *just* a black girl. Okay?"

He nodded slowly. "I'm starting to realize that." It was the truth. He'd had an entire week to come to the conclusion that Larke wasn't *just* another girl he wanted to fuck. She was…different. How different? He was working on figuring that out.

She peered into his face, her eyes searching. "Really, Chase? Because we can't be friends if you're going to keep referring to me like that. Or view me as inferior. I can tell you now, it won't work at all."

Friends?

Chase arched his brows. "I never said anything about us being friends."

Larke shifted on the seat beside him. "Then what do you expect? I mean, usually relationships, attraction starts out with people being friends. Well sort of friends, I would imagine. I thought that's what you wanted by showing me the necklace. That we could be friends now?"

He chuckled softly. "I was eleven, Larke. Friendship is all I could've had with a girl. That's not what I want with you."

She chewed on her bottom lip, looking almost scared again. For a second he was afraid she'd move away from him. Reject the faintest suggestion of being with him. She didn't. Chase let out the breath of relief he hadn't realized he'd been holding in.

"I'm not sure I can offer you anything more than friendship. I'm no longer afraid of you. So you're wrong on that part. I need some time to process all of this. You said I had you feeling messed up, but how do you think I feel right now? I never expected any of this—for the two of us to sit here, pretending like there's nothing in between us."

"*Would* it be bad if we did a little pretending?"

She shot him a pained smile. "I don't know. Pretending might work, but the question is for how long." She shook her head then. "No. That wouldn't work for us. I don't need you to pretend. All I want is for you to see me for who I am, Larke Justine Taylor." Her smile widened, reaching all the way to her eyes—eyes he was beginning to find prettier and prettier by the second. "A girl who was named after a bird."

Chase grinned, noting how Larke's entire face seemed to light up with her smile still in place. "It's a cute name. It fits you."

"Thanks," she said shyly, welding her gaze to his.

His cheeks grow hot under her stare. What was he, twenty-four or eleven? Chase cleared his throat. Back to business. "What you said before, about not pretending. I don't want to either." He exhaled a deep breath. "As for what I said earlier—I didn't mean it the way it came out. I know it might be hard to believe, really hard actually, but I don't have a problem with you being black. I don't see you as my enemy or anything like that. To be honest, when I look at you, I see the girl who shared her candy and sweater with me when I didn't deserve it. More than that, I see a woman I'd like to be with. Friendship, whatever you wanna call it, as long as it'll make you feel comfortable with me."

Chapter Five

For hours and well into the next day on the drive down to Jacksonville, Chase played and replayed his last conversation with Larke inside his head. She'd agreed to give him a chance. That in itself made him feel as if he'd accomplished the impossible, which also gave him hope that he might be able to do another impossible feat—keep himself from strangling McNair. The shaved-head man was seated next to Chase inside a seedy bar down the street from the motel they'd chosen for the night.

Chase wasn't a big drinker despite the glass of Jägermeister in his hand. Drinking took control away. He'd seen it happen with his grandfather, Trevor, and his mother. Truth be told, drinking too much wasn't restricted to his immediate family. Alcoholism was becoming a source of problem with some members of Antebellum Resistance. In between talks of a Zionist controlled media and government, coupled with the vital need to preserve white racial identity; many nationalists numbed their anger and frustration the easiest way they knew how. Alcohol, or shooting up and snorting meth, the drug that was most available and was almost as easy as bread to obtain among white supremacists.

Tonight was the first night Chase wished he was on something. Anything to cool down, fuck, even completely get rid of his newfound obsession with Larke. He wanted her and God knew he was going to have her, but damn... The last thing he needed was anything or anyone coming between him and his commitments.

Taking a swig of the beer, he caught sight of one of the two women who'd approached him minutes ago. The blonde had been decent enough, the type of girl he would've had no problem spending a couple of hours with. Nice figure, clean, dressed all right, not too slutty. She'd stood beside him running her fingertips along the length of his arm, openly admiring the same tattoos that had put the look of fear and disgust on Larke's face.

Overcome with annoyance and anger directed at himself *and* the woman for touching him in the first place, Chase had brushed her hand aside while mumbling something that probably came out as a 'fuck off'.

"Hudson, what the hell's wrong with you tonight?"

Chase glanced up from the rim of his glass to face McNair, who was eyeing him with caution. "You told that hot blonde over there to fuck off."

"Then buy her a drink if you feel sorry for her."

"Not my taste. Breasts looked fake. Anyways, I thought you and Haley were supposed to be fucking?"

Wait, what? He'd never so much as kissed the girl. Hell, his one phone call to her had been a mistake. "Did you hear that piece of bullshit at your latest tea party?" Chase curled his lips and faced the other man. "Seriously, is that what you do each day, sit back and gossip like a bitch?"

McNair shrugged. "Gotta pass the day somehow besides getting glassed. Not all of us can sit back knowing we got a ship sailing out there, bringing in some cash."

Chase scowled. They'd grown up together and McNair must have conveniently forgotten that while Chase was working every day, he and his friends were too busy trying to make a name for themselves by starting trouble with minorities, for the hell of it.

Matter of fact, Chase wondered if McNair remembered the last time he tried to fuck with him, making jokes about his absent mother.

Taking another swig of beer, Chase decided to ignore the man for the remainder of the evening. It would be senseless to bring attention to himself inside the bar, risking trouble with the law and have Larke think worse of him than she already did.

With McNair and his issues out of sight, out of mind, Chase turned to the television. Any wishful thinking of getting glassed– as McNair had put it–was put to rest. There wasn't a drug strong enough to dull his mind from thoughts of Larke.

A commercial came on the large mounted screen. Normally he wouldn't pay any attention since he didn't even have a TV in his house but this advertisement stood out. Not because Chase was interested in the product they were selling. No. It was the loud exaggerated snort that came from McNair's reaction to the commercial that made him watch it.

On the screen was a woman—a black woman who was the same complexion as Larke. Maybe a shade lighter. The woman appears frustrated, cleaning up while her husband and his buddies sat around the couch watching football and eating chips. It's a beer commercial and Chase knew there was a point in there somewhere, but it wasn't important.

McNair laughed. "Would'da had that one outside in the fields." With overblown self-importance, he continued, "Pick my cotton faster, bitch." He turned to Chase, his tone powered with the confidence of knowing that inside this bar he could openly make references to slavery without judgment. "What do you think is worse, them trying to say low-class *negroes* like those fools can live in a house that big or the white race traitors sitting around with the husband laughing and eating from the same bowl of chips?"

McNair snorted again and shook his head as if Chase had given him the answer he wanted. But Chase couldn't reply. Speech left him. His entire body grew tense, coiled like a spring ready to snap.

The slave comment threw him for a loop. He wasn't dumb. Of course he knew all about slavery. His ancestors had fought to keep it. Gramps would brag, his voice bursting with pride at the effort of the Confederacy to preserve the practice. Chase had been proud too. Still was? He didn't know.

Hearing McNair say it like that, though... Those words could've come from his own mouth. Before he'd found himself wanting a certain girl whose skin color meant back in those times, she would've been worthy of nothing better than toiling outside in the fields.

He pushed his glass of beer aside. What could he say to McNair when he was no better? He'd be a hypocrite. Chase kept his mouth closed. The bartender cast a nervous glance between them. Flinging a towel over his shoulder, the gray-haired man issued them a lukewarm smile. "Sorry about that. I don't have control over the crap those liberals put on television these days. No channel's safe, huh?"

Chase eyed the man quizzically, wondering if he meant those words or was attempting to appease him and McNair. *Gotta keep the psycho white supremacists happy, right?*

"I'm done for the night," Chase bit out. He slapped a couple of bills on the counter and returned to the motel. The room was passable. Clean without any nasty stench or insects running about. Not a complete dump. He was used to staying in motels like this ever since his grandfather began taking him all over the country to meet with other nationalists. Driving long stretches, sleeping in cheap motels that would ensure they never left much of a paper trail leading to their influential supporters or those wishing to join the cause.

The motel was also the perfect place to stay, seeing as how he'd stupidly agreed to let Trevor use his ship for another one of his lame ass dealings. Old Joe Butler was probably rolling over in his grave, knowing how desperate things were becoming that they'd resorted to smuggling liquor to make sure enough funds were available to pay out the monthly checks to each AR household living in Lee's Fortress.

The 'stipend' as his grandfather and Trevor had referred to it when they'd first rolled out the idea, was an experiment aimed at drawing in more members. If the government was more concerned about pleasing and helping everyone except whites, then AR would be the first group to actively provide financial support to its members. Those living in Lee's Fortress were the guinea pigs, the ones who would be grateful enough that they recruited anyone who was teetering on the side of nationalism. Not only that, they were also now at the beck and call of Trevor and his underlings. Underlings like himself.

For now.

On that thought, Chase wondered what Larke would think if she knew the inner workings of the movement he'd been born into. Years ago, she'd been shocked by the things he'd told her. Not being allowed to watch television, rarely eating things like candy, ice cream and other typical snacks meant for children because his mother never trusted what the manufacturers were putting in them.

Larke had been especially shocked that he'd never tasted a Snickers bar before. She'd told him so as they'd sat on the damp ground with the aftertaste of sugar and chocolate on their tongues. Chase groaned, his thoughts immediately shifting. She'd probably taste so damn sweet. Her lips, tongue, between her legs… Yes, he'd definitely want to taste Larke's pussy.

Tracing a hand across his jaw, Chase drew in a ragged breath. His cock hardened, moisture gathering at the tip, a warning that he needed to cool it before he ended up ejaculating inside the motel room. All alone. Another deep breath. He switched on the television, desperate for distraction. There was none. No matter what, all he could see was Larke; with her lips full, ripe and utterly kissable. Talking to him. Smiling at him.

He turned off the TV, staring at the black screen, knowing the only thing he needed was the sound of her voice. Warm with a raspy undertone. When she spoke, it was unlike anything he'd ever heard on another female. Sexy as hell, although he doubted she realized it. His head swam with images of Larke lying in his bed, naked and willing, moaning his name in between breathless pants as he buried himself deep, filling her to the brim.

Weakened by his need to talk with her, Chase picked up his phone, uncaring how late it was. If those tender looks Larke had given him in the park yesterday meant anything, she'd definitely want to hear his voice too. She'd understand why he'd call so late— that all he wanted was some kind of reassurance that he was still on her mind.

She answered on the second ring. An unnamed emotion unfurled inside his chest at her gentle, feminine greeting. He chose not to think about or analyze the feeling. It was too much right now.

"Chase?"

"It's me."

"You sound tired," she pointed out. "What's going on?"

"Not much. Is it bad that I called this late?" He just remembered he hadn't told her he'd be out of state today.

"It's okay. I wasn't sleeping or anything. Are you at your home?"

"No. Why'd you ask?"

"The connection sounded kind of weird. Where are you?"

"Florida. Jacksonville actually."

"Oh." He'd surprised her. Would she begin to interrogate him? Make assumptions?

"Is everything okay?"

"Everything's good. Aren't you wondering what I'm doing down here?" he asked, baffled she wasn't flinging a barrage of questions at him.

She laughed. "Well yeah. Of course. But it's late. I was kind of leery of you telling me something that would make it hard for me to sleep tonight. I guess that's not the case. So, tell me, Chase Hudson, what are you doing in Jacksonville of all places?"

"Work," he said, smiling to himself at her playfulness. "Plain boring work. Not the kind of work you're probably imagining. Swear to God. I came down here to meet with the new captain of a ship I own. It's sailing out tomorrow afternoon."

"Truly?"

"Yeah." His smile turned into a grin. "I don't look like a bum or anything. I mean, I try my best not to. Didn't you wonder if I had a job?"

She laughed again. "I did, but I don't know. I guess all the other stuff just kind of overshadowed it. Maybe I even thought that *was* your full-time job."

Chase would've laughed too if there hadn't been a ring of truth to what she said. And if he hadn't detected the hint of caution in her voice. While he *was* technically on the payroll for random things he did for the group, the fact that she'd correctly assumed that his entire life revolved around white supremacy made his stomach churn. It shouldn't but it did.

"How's your book coming along?" he asked, shifting the focus off himself.

"It's going great. I'm in the middle of a new story. My head cleared a lot after our talk yesterday."

"It wasn't clear before?"

She became silent. Seconds ticked by before she quietly confessed, "No, it wasn't. I was actually a bit disturbed after seeing you for the first time in so many years. I wasn't sure how to feel. You have to understand it was a shock seeing the real you as opposed to how I'd imagined you." She sighed. "I guess I just confessed to thinking about you over the years. It's fine. I'm not embarrassed to admit I always wondered how you were."

Chase took no offense at the word disturbed. It was to be expected. But Jesus… Larke had thought about him all this time?

He considered asking if he had disappointed her but decided against it, fearing the answer. "How do you feel now?"

"Happy. I'm glad we reconnected in spite of everything. I liked talking with you yesterday. More than I should've." There was a brief moment of quietness before she added, "I'd actually like to see you again." He heard an intake of breath, followed by another pause. "As long as you don't use any racist slurs to me or in front of me."

His gut twisted again. This time it felt like someone had taken a knife and began slashing at his innards. Swallowing hard, Chase whispered, "I can do that. I can't promise one or two won't slip out, but they wouldn't be directed at you." Shit. He cleared his throat and tried again. "I mean I'll try real hard to watch what I say."

"Thank you."

Chase nodded, suddenly feeling lower than the underbelly of a snake. Larke was thanking him for something people weren't supposed to get thanked for. Being decent. Respectful.

"Would you like to hear what I have so far?"

Chase blinked. Focusing, he realized she was talking about her book. "Yeah, sure."

"It's meant for three and four-year-olds. Not too long and the plus side is, it *might* just put you to sleep. So, this is a win-win deal."

His lips eased into a smile, which was real easy to do when talking to her. "Bring it. But if it's cheesy, I'm gonna let you know, right?"

"I'd be angry if you didn't."

She began reading and Chase listened until she let out a whoosh of air and said, "And that's all I have for now."

As they'd agree, he told her his opinion of the main character in her story. She agreed with him. But what surprised him the most was that she ended up asking if he had a suggestion on how she could fix the character in her book.

That was new.

Larke was the only person he could think of who gave a damn about his opinion. He was used to doing, not advising. Doing what he was told, or asked after a bit of buttering up. That's what everyone expected of him.

Annoyed that he'd allowed AR to slip into his thoughts, Chase quickly dragged his mind from the group. That kind of business had no place inside his head when talking to Larke. He opened his mouth, on the verge of asking her what she was wearing. He clamped it shut. Too much. Too soon. Not wishing to scare her off, he settled on asking the one thing that had been on his mind all day long. "Can I see you after I get home?"

"When are you coming back?"

"I'm driving home tomorrow evening."

"You won't be too tired?"

Too tired to see her? Never. "I'm good. I've been driving across the states since before I got my license. No big deal."

"Okay." Another pause. "Can I ask you something? It might seem stupid and I suppose I already know the answer—"

He cut off her nervous rambling. "What do you wanna know?"

"Have you ever been with *any* non-white person?"

"Inside the same building? Yes. Slept with? No, if that's what you want to know." He frowned. "Why did you ask?"

"I was doing some thinking last night. I knew some kids from high school whose parents were pretty strict; never letting them have a single taste of alcohol because they hadn't reached twenty-one. When they went away to college, many of them spent their time partying and drinking. They went pretty crazy with this new freedom. That memory led me to wonder—could it be like that for you? You were raised to believe being with someone outside of your race is bad. What if you see me as a safe choice to kind of test the waters, see what all this forbidden drama is really about?" She inhaled. "I'm not sure if what I'm saying makes much sense. Maybe I'm just confused with all this stuff going on inside my head. Then again, your attraction to me probably hasn't gone that far for this sort of thinking."

"It has," Chase murmured into the phone. "It's gone real far." So much, that his cock shot rock hard at the faintest possibility of them being intimate. Chase brushed his hand over his erection as it swelled painfully. "You're not crazy. I've already thought about everything you said. I had a lot of time to. All last week when I was wondering what my next move was gonna be. Those same thoughts ran through my mind. But it's not like that. For starters, there's nothing safe about the way you have me feeling. I've never been nervous around any girl except you. I'm also not attracted to you because I have fantasies of being with a black girl. Never had. It's just you I want. The girl with the pretty round face and laugh that made me forget who I was."

Chapter Six

Larke played the scenario inside her head a hundred times over. She'd been a nervous wreck ever since their last conversation. It wasn't that she didn't want to see Chase. It was a matter of how *much* she wanted to see him, without making a fool of herself. She twirled a braid around her fingertip. Why oh why hadn't she taken the time to date more and gain experience in not behaving like a complete idiot, whose palms were already sweating with fear and excitement.

Not a single book on her shelf could give Larke advice on how to stay calm after hearing everything he had to say last night. She was glad they'd hung up shortly after Chase mentioned her laughter and what it did to him. Keeping her voice from trembling had been so hard once it hit her that perhaps her first impression of him had been too harsh. There was nothing monstrous about him. While Chase was definitely a victim of his parentage and upbringing, there was a good chance he was simply a man too afraid to change his ways.

The knock on her door caused her stomach to tighten into knots and bows. Drawing in a deep breath, Larke peeked through the peephole with one hand on the doorknob. Once again, she was face to face with the man occupying almost every junction of her mind. Chase stood at her doorway in a pair of dark blue jeans and another long-sleeved shirt. She hadn't wanted to admit it before but he was very handsome. When she'd first seen him, the thought had struck her deep inside but it had felt wrong, taboo for viewing someone with his beliefs in terms of looks.

She watched as he strode inside her apartment, cautiously looking around. For a second, Larke wondered if he'd expected her place to be... Well, she wasn't sure. Maybe completely decorated with African art and all the black related paraphernalia anyone could think of. There was a painting of a giraffe on the wall, but the rest were of various landscapes around the world. Nothing special.

Feeling awkward, she shifted her eyes, watching his face. Chase lowered his head, meeting her stare.

Breathe.

Her body refused to obey. The breath lodged at the base of her throat as he eased toward her, his heated gaze holding her captive. "You still look like you're afraid of me."

Larke shook her head, pushing away a braid that fell to the side of her face. "I'm not."

Chase inched closer. So close she was able to see the edge of one of his many tattoos snaking out the neckline of his shirt. Cocking his head to the side, he stroked his rough fingertip across her chin. "I hope you're telling me the truth. I don't care what other people think of me. If I make people afraid. You and me, though... That's something else. Don't ever worry that I'll hurt you. I won't, Larke. I swear to everything that's holy, I'd never put my hands on you in any way that would harm you." He expelled a ragged breath, holding out in his hands. "Look, I even make sure to keep my arms covered when I'm around you. I'm trying not to do anything that's gonna upset you."

Tenderness blossomed in her. So, *that's* why he'd worn the long-sleeved shirt that morning in the park despite the high temperature.

"I'm sorry," Larke whispered. "I want you here and I've been waiting to see you all this time. It's just that I'm not used to having anyone inside my apartment. No one except for my friend, Riva, who you saw at the bowling alley that evening."

He smiled at her. "You don't have anything to be sorry about. I can't believe you even invited me in here." He glanced around the room, his vision landing on a copy of her latest book.

"Can I look at it?"

Larke nodded then reached for the book, handing it to him. She used the time to study him as he flipped through the pages. At one point, Chase raised his head, staring at her with…awe. Her cheeks grew hot beneath his stare, as if they were on fire. The harsh plains of his angular face appeared softer as he lowered his gaze and continued reading. Another minute passed before he placed it back on the shelf.

The children's book, however, was no longer on Larke's mind. Despite her pride, that accomplishment was the last thing she wanted to discuss. The overwhelming need to touch Chase, run her hands along his face and down the length of his muscular frame made her heart slam wildly against her ribcage. And most of all, her fingers itched to help him out of that long-sleeved shirt, so out of place in the sweltering summer night.

Larke eased toward him, only to step back and jump as the timer in the kitchen went off. Its beep was shrill and jarring. Her eyes widened. She slapped her palm against her forehead. "Oh my God. I almost forgot the food."

Racing into the kitchen, she grabbed two pot holders and removed the baked chicken from the oven.

"You do eat chicken, don't you?" she asked while sprinkling Parmesan cheese over the golden crust. "Or is that a no go?"

"Chicken is fine. Didn't know you'd be cooking."

"It was a spur of the moment decision. I figured you'd need

something proper to eat after driving for so long. None of that McDonald's stuff."

He laughed, the sound low and deep. "You got something against fast food?"

"The opposite. If I start to eat one fry I'll end up eating the entire box." She checked the pot of broccoli rice pilaf on the stove then turned to face him. "You remember how I was before. These days I try to be more careful with what I eat." She quirked her lips to downplay her sudden embarrassment in not being skinny. "This is also my warning that if we ever get trapped anywhere together, you won't find a stash of candy inside my bag." Larke chuckled at her own silliness then stopped altogether, noticing the set firmness of Chase's jaws.

He was staring at her, his eyes raking over her face, breasts, and hips. She immediately regretted mentioning her weight. Her stomach fluttered as he inclined his head, indicating that he had concluded his scrutiny of her body. "I thought I already told you you looked good?" His voice was gruff and his brows rose as if he awaited an answer. Trapped beneath his intense gaze, Larke managed a nod. She wondered if he'd meant his comment from outside the bowling alley about growing into her fat. "I suppose you did."

"If you want me to say it again, I will."

"You don't have to repeat anything," she insisted. "I was being silly and truthful, not fishing for compliments."

In a matter of seconds, before she could anticipate his move, Chase was across the room standing beside her in the kitchen. "I didn't think you were fishing. What you said only gave me an excuse to let you know what I think. You don't need to do a damn thing to make yourself different or thinner. You're perfect, Larke. Honest to God." He curled his finger around a long braid, slowly allowing it to uncoil and tumble onto her chest.

Her nipples tightened and beaded underneath his attentive stare. She dabbed her tongue over her lips. Her blood felt hot, coursing through her body and roaring inside her ears. Chase's eyes grew hazy, his lips curved into a half smile.

Larke quivered. He *knew* she was aroused. She closed her eyes as he rasped, "It'd be a shame if you had a problem with those breasts of yours. Bet they look so fucking good underneath that shirt."

Liquid heat flooded her lower belly. Larke moaned inside her head at the shameless feel of her sex clenching and tightening for the unknown. No man had ever said such things to her before. Desire clouded her reasoning, leading her to confess a lack of experience. "I haven't dated much so I haven't dealt with a lot of men. Any man really if I'm being honest. But what you said to me—I liked hearing it." Larke sighed. "I guess I'm saying all this because I wanted you to know I've never been alone and so close with anyone before."

He searched her face. "Are you trying to tell me you've never been with a man before?"

"Yes." Her pulse raced at his insistent stare of disbelief. "You think I'm weird don't you?"

He shrugged. "Nothing weird about being a virgin."

Larke let out a small cough, averting her gaze. "We, um... We should eat before the food gets cold."

Chase helped to bring the food out of the kitchen and onto the dining room table. "You're a good cook," he said, in between bites of the chicken. "Best food I've had since…." He crinkled his forehead. "Since I can remember, really."

Larke smiled to herself. She was flattered, but honestly, she wasn't *that* good of a cook. "Don't you eat at restaurants?"

He shook his head, chuckling with a measure of self-derision. "No. That's not really my sort of thing. I can cook just fine. When I don't feel like it, we have certain restaurants that deliver to the area." He ate another morsel of the meat. "Their food's all right. Nothing like this, though."

"Okay. Since I now know you're not big on going out to eat, what exactly do you enjoy doing in your spare time?"

"Hunting," he said, eyeing her carefully. "Shouldn't surprise you, I guess."

It didn't. "Apart from hunting, what else do you like?" Larke asked.

Chase lifted a shoulder and scratched his brow. "Not much else. Sometimes I carve knives."

She thought back to the one he'd had while chasing her. It *had* looked a bit crude and not professionally made. "Did you make the knife I saw you with before?"

"Yeah" he answered, lowering his head. "That one I definitely made."

"What else do you carve?"

He paused, slowly raising his face to look at her. Surprise filtered into his lackluster eyes. Did Chase think she wouldn't want to continue talking to him because of that memory? Shrugging, he said, "Nothing important. Just stupid stuff." A moment passed and then his brows furrowed with suspicion. "Why the sudden interest?"

Larke pursed her lip. "I wanted to know more about you. That's all. But if it makes you uncomfortable we can talk about something else."

He visibly relaxed. "Sorry. It doesn't. I'm just not used to small talk or anyone wanting to know what I like and all. Might take some getting used to."

Anyone. Did that include his mother and stepfather? Surely even the most hardened racist took pride in their children and loved them. She wanted to ask about his family but decided against. Too many questions might put Chase on the offensive.

After the meal ended, Larke rose to clear the table. Chase did the same, helping in spite of her insistence that it wasn't necessary.

"I thought maybe we could watch a movie if you're in the mood," she suggested, putting the last of the dishes in the dishwasher.

"Sounds like a plan."

"Is there anything in particular you'd like to see?"

He shook his head. "It doesn't matter. As long as it doesn't involve singing, teenage vampires or wedding dresses, I'm good."

Larke laughed as she went to the television screen. "Then we dislike the same things." She scrolled down the menu. "I'll add watching movies to my list of Chase's likes. What about comedy films?"

"They're okay. I've seen a couple of them. Mostly when I'm out of town inside a motel room. Kills time. I don't have a television at home and didn't have one growing up, so never really caught on to TV watching."

"As nonchalant as possible, Larke asked, "I take it not all of these trips had anything to do with your shipping business?"

His face immediately closed up. His eyes glinted with a warning. "Let's watch the movie, okay?"

Nodding slowly, she clicked play and sat beside him. "It's a Will Smith movie. You know who that is right?" She pursed her lips. "Or would you prefer something else? There's an old Clint Eastwood western I saw with my dad once. It was pretty good. We could watch that instead if you'd like."

He shook his head. "The movie's fine. I've seen Independence Day. It's all good. No worries."

Chapter Seven

Chase felt the exact moment Larke let her guard down. One minute she was laughing, the next she was leaning over until finally, her head came to rest on his shoulder. In that moment it felt as if he was eleven all over again with Larke invading his personal space as they fell asleep together.

The only difference was, this time his body was reacting. His cock twitching, gearing up for her touch. He wanted to draw her into his arms, real tight and… And nothing. Chase ran his hand over his jaw. As much as he wanted to be close to Larke, he knew none of that was going to happen. She'd already made it clear that she'd never slept with a man. Deep down he wondered if she'd told it to him as some kind of warning to keep his dirty thoughts in check.

"It was good, wasn't it?" she asked, raising her head from his shoulder.

What was good? Chase searched his mind for a clue to what she was talking about. Oh. He was supposed to have been focused on the movie and not her. "It was interesting. Can't say too much about the ending, though."

Her lips spread into a crooked smile. Almost like she knew his secret—that he'd spent the majority of time sneaking glances at her instead of watching the movie. Her gaze suddenly switched to the clock on the living room wall. He followed it, taking note that the time was nearing ten-thirty.

Larke stared at him. She nibbled her bottom lip then brought her attention back to the clock. Figuring he'd worn out his welcome, Chase racked his brain for the right thing to say. He opened his mouth but was unable to stifle the yawn that snuck out in place of the words he meant to use. Tiredness from driving so many hours home, freshening up then rushing across town to see the girl he couldn't stop thinking about hit him like a blow.

"Chase?"

"Hmm."

"You're very tired, aren't you?"

Yep. Very. He straightened to his feet. "A little. I actually wanted to thank you for the food and everything before I head out."

Her brows furrowed although she was no longer watching the clock. "You've been driving pretty much all day to get home." Her eyes appeared darker, worried. But why? He was leaving.

She continued. "I don't think watching the movie was such a good idea. Now you have another half an hour to Lee's Fortress. I'm not suggesting anything. Okay, I am. The thing is, I don't think it's the safest idea for you to drive home right now. I'd hate for something to happen. If anything were to happen, it would be because you came here to see me."

Every nerve cell inside his body stood on edge. So that explained her nervous glances at the clock. She was worried about him. Larke—a *black* female who knew about his twisted beliefs had no problem showing concern for him. Staggered by the revelation, Chase felt his chest tighten.

"What are you suggesting?" he asked, his tone rougher than intended because of the lump inside his throat.

"That you spend the night here." She smiled. "To show you what a nice person I am, I'll even let you sleep on my bed. I can take the couch because, well… She waved her hand in the air, gesturing toward his body. "You're like a mountain."

He *was* much bigger than her at around six feet three inches and well over two hundred pounds of solid muscle from lifting iron in his 'spare time' as Larke would've called it.

The lump in his throat felt bigger. He didn't deserve her concern or that look in her eyes. The tenderness. He didn't deserve a lick of it at all.

"That's real nice of you, Larke. Means a lot, to be honest, but I can't stay."

Her eyes searched his own, staring so deep Chase wondered if she could see everything he tried to hide. Once again, the all-consuming need to take her into his arms took a hold of him. He wanted to hold her close, inhale her scent–flowers and sweetness–then bury himself so deep inside her lush body. Why? For no other reason than it felt *right*. Like being near this woman was the only thing good and worthy in his life.

She pressed her hand to his chest. His breath stopped. All the muscles inside of him went still. "Larke?" Chase covered her hand with his. "What's going on here, angel? Why are you being so sweet to me?"

"I don't know," she whispered, gazing up at him with eyes big and full of promises. "I'm just treating you normal. How you should be treated. The way I'd want to be treated. You tell me you can't stay, but I don't want you to go. Not yet. And it's not only because I'm worried about you."

Before he had a chance to speak, she lowered her hand and beckoned, "Come here."

In a daze, Chase followed behind her. They rounded a corner and entered her bedroom. In the middle of the room was a queen-sized bed, complete with a colorful, eye-gouging floral comforter. A notebook and pen rested on her bedside table.

"I wanted to show you where the room is." She gave him a

mischievous grin. "Since, you know, we've decided you're staying and all."

Chase looked at her and was unable to contain the smile on his lips. They both knew he hadn't decided a damn thing. This was her sly way of giving him an order.

"I agreed?"

She flickered her tongue across her lip and nodded. Mesmerized by the subtle yet erotic action, Chase lowered his head, ignoring the siren blaring inside his mind, warning him to back away. Larke must have sensed his intention-his need, because she raised her head at the same time.

Moaning softly, she parted her lips, allowing him to slip inside, exploring the taste of her mouth. Larke curled her fingers around his arm, mewling in the back of her throat.

The kiss broke as they both came up for air. Inside his chest, his heart pounded like the beating of a sledgehammer, vibrating throughout his entire body. Swallowing hard, Chase staggered backward, holding Larke at arm's length. It was the only thing he could do to prevent himself from throwing her across her neatly-made bed, spreading her thighs and sliding into her in one swift thrust.

Fuck. Chase gulped in some air, shoved a hand through his hair. His mind was a complete mess because he could *still* taste her on his lips. All innocence and tender sweetness. Things he shouldn't have. Had never wanted. His skin tingled where her fingertips had closed around him. His dick… He brought a fist to his mouth and sucked in a deep breath. Larke and her moaning had him stiff and hurting so damn much.

"I'm sorry," she whispered. She traced her index finger across her lips. "I–I don't know what to say. Chase, this wasn't about sex. I only brought you here to show you the room. Nothing more. I swear. I'm really sorry. After everything I said, I'd hate for you to think I'm playing with you. I'd never do that."

Larke looked as affected as he felt. Her braids were disheveled and her lips slightly swollen. She was even sweeping her pink tongue over her lips. Did she realize what she was doing? He gulped in another breath. "You liked it?"

She stared at him wide-eyed. He could see the pulse in her neck fluttering like crazy as she nodded. Her lips eased into a delicate smile. "It was wonderful." She narrowed her brows, "What about you? I mean. Are we okay? Did you like kissing me, or was it..." She bit her lip and averted her gaze, letting the rest of her question hang in the air.

Chase's gut clenched. He was fully aware of what she was trying to ask without being able to finish the painful sentence. He managed a nod then dipped his head, capturing her lips between his own to show her the truth.

"Had to do it," he murmured when the kiss ended. He tapped the corner of her lips with his thumb. "You're addicting."

"So are you."

His entire body felt warm and alive as her words washed over him. In that moment, Chase knew it was too late for him to leave and too late to ever go anywhere but forward in this relationship.

Larke continued to hold him in her view, her gaze lowering to his chest, arms and toward his legs. Her brows wrinkled like they did earlier. "Do you—" She stopped, shook her head and allowed her hand to fall at her side. "Nevermind. I'll grab some clothes and go out in the living room."

Chase grabbed her hand, pulling her back. "Don't do this, Larke. You wanted to ask me something. I know it had to be important to you. What was it? What do you wanna know?"

"I was curious about something but it doesn't matter. I'm not sure it would make a difference anyway."

"Tell me."

She gave him a pained stare then rushed out, "Do you have the tattoos all over your body?"

Chase shook his head. Drawing in a breath, he peeled the shirt over his head, half afraid of her reaction, but understanding her concern. He needed to be upfront about everything, including the tattoos. "I don't have anything on my legs. Only what you see here on my upper body."

She nodded slowly. Her gaze traveled over his chest, stomach, and arms. Closing his eyes, Chase turned, knowing she needed to see it all. Shame dug into him as he pictured her reaction while reading the words splayed on his back. 'Crazy White Boy', a term identifying him as a white supremacist, along with the other nationalist symbols that had meaning to him. He prayed she didn't recognize the majority of them or understood what they stood for.

Scrutiny completed, Larke turned to him and quietly said, "I thought maybe you had a swastika."

He shook his head, glad he'd refused that tattoo while some his friends opted to have it inked onto their skin. "My grandfather always said the Nazi party ruined the image of white nationalism. Made people lose respect for our beliefs and cause."

"Okay. But please tell me you agree what they did to the Jewish people was horrendous."

Her eyes were imploring him again, testing out his humanity. "Larke…"

Sighing loudly, she tightened her jaw then returned her attention to the rest of his tattoos. "I *do* recognize some of these symbols. Not all, but quite a few." She pressed her fingertip to a spot on his shoulder. Chase felt her hand move, tracing the ones she claimed to recognize. He stood, silently letting her explore and examine all the wicked parts of him. The ones she can only see on the outside. Look for herself and decide if she can allow herself to belong and maybe one day open her body to a monster like himself.

"It hurts to see these things," she said, not a hint of anger in her tone. "But I think… No. I *know* and believe this with all my heart, that you're not a horrible person. I just need you to tell me that somewhere deep inside, you know there's a lot of wrong in many of the things I'm seeing here." She touched a spot above his chest. "Like this one." Her fingertip grazed the Confederate flag standing high amid flames and ashes. "Put yourself in my shoes, Chase, then tell me if you understand."

He did. Hell, he couldn't get McNair's fucking snort out of his head, laughing and talking about the woman in the beer commercial. Ever since that night, he'd had time to reflect on his thoughts or rather his *lack* of real thoughts on certain issues. It wasn't that he actually believed black people should be slaves or should've been enslaved in the first place. No one should have the right to own another person. At least not in terms of property for forced labor.

Chase pinched the bridge of his nose, unaware that his head hung low until he felt Larke's arm circling his neck in a delicate embrace.

He raised his head and recalled her previous question about the Jews. "No. I don't agree with what happened."

Her arms tightened around him. All he could feel next was her lips on his shoulder, warming his skin. A groan slipped from his mouth before he could silence it.

"Shh." Her dark eyes peered up at him. Larke lowered her head again, sprinkling hot kisses along his chest and each and every one of the tattoos she despised. When her lips stroked the words on his arm, Chase jumped, losing his cool.

Shit. Shit. Shit.

He rubbed the top of his head, back and forth. Crazed. Did Larke know what she was doing to him? His chest clenched and expanded. His lungs felt as if someone was squeezing the air from them. The back of his eyelids burned. Actually stung with tears. He never cried. Wouldn't cry.

"It's okay." She soothed him by rubbing her cheek along his arm, her skin coming into contact with so much hate. "Honestly,

Chase. It's fine. We have each other now. We can deal with this together."

He was powerless to her—a female half his size who had the kind of strength he could only dream of having or understanding.

Larke moved to the bed, patted a spot beside her and said, "Turn over." Chase did just that, lying on his stomach. Craning his head, he saw her kneeling at his side. He meant to ask what she had in mind but there was no need. With a tiny grin on her face, Larke steepled her fingers and flexed her hands. He stifled a groan as she began caressing then massaging his shoulder blades. Smooth fingertips dug into his back, easing the coiled tension in his muscles.

No one had ever given him a massage. Then again, he couldn't imagine allowing any of the women he'd fucked to get that close to him. So much touching for no good reason. With Larke…he craved her touch like nothing else. It didn't have to be sexual, although if he was being honest, her fingers delving into his hard flesh, kneading and massaging; felt like a close second to the pleasure of kissing her. Close, because the only thing that could ever top having his lips on hers was lowering himself between her thighs and plunging all the way to the hilt.

"Better?" She was leaning over and smiling. Thin braids fell against the side of her face.

Chase rolled over on the bed and grazed her cheek with the back of his hand. His heart felt as if it was wedged somewhere between his chest and the top of his throat.

Fuck it to hell! He was falling for Larke. She had blindsided him, throwing a curve in the path he was on. He had no idea if she realized the effect she was having on him, lying there with her face propped against her palm, gazing at him as if he was someone special.

"I've never met anyone like you," Chase told her, unable to hold back.

"Is that good or bad?"

"Good. And bad. Real bad actually."

The spark of light inside her eyes faded. All traces of happiness melted from her face. "Oh." She shifted away from him, intent on putting distance between them. Chase wouldn't allow it. He closed his arm around her waist, stilling her movement. "Stay beside me. All I'm trying to tell you is, you're different. I don't mean because you're black. Just that you're the nicest person I know. You had so many reasons to hate and push me away, but you haven't. You're also so damn pretty it makes my head hurts. I like being around you, Larke and when I'm not around you, I'm thinking about you all the time."

She stared at him in confusion. "What's the bad part?"

"Everything I said. I wasn't raised for anything like this to happen. You and me—we shouldn't even be talking. Much less me lying on your bed hoping I can kiss you again. Do you understand what I'm trying to tell you?"

"I get it," she said quietly. "You've changed your mind about us being together."

Was she serious? Yes, common sense was yelling at him to change his mind, but any chance of that happening was impossible now. Larke had to know that. Why else would he have rushed over here to see her? He was in neck deep, with wanting her. Everything about her was drawing him in.

She put her lips on my tattoos.

His skin shivered. Chase shook his head quickly, issuing a firm, "No. I didn't change my mind. I want you. That's not gonna stop anytime soon." Frustrated, he let out a loud sigh. How could he fully explain it without frightening her again?

The two of them in a relationship would piss off a lot of people. The hatred ran deep. He'd seen it, was actively living and participating in it. Race traitors were the worst of the worst. He wasn't allowed to join the ranks of those who'd given up or abandoned the movement to make America a haven for white people—like it used to be.

Chase was supposed to lead, not set them behind. If anyone found about him and Larke, he knew he'd be 'forgiven'. They'd view it as a mistake. Explain the relationship away as a moment of weakness brought on by liberal brainwashing or a that he was simply a loyal nationalist who became overcome by grotesque curiosity for the unknown. He knew the last one would be the easiest for everyone to accept.

The real problem, however, was Larke. She'd be seen as the filthy ni–. He shut his eyes. Thinking that word was difficult and painful now that he understood how much it bothered her. They'd see her as the disgusting minority who'd figured out a way to tempt one of their own. And the real fanatics–the same ones terrified of leaving Lee's Fortress–might even attempt to harm her.

Chase stared at Larke. She appeared hesitant. He leaned over and brushed his lips against hers. "I'm not going anywhere. I only wanted you to understand that being with you isn't something I'm taking lightly."

He really wasn't. Larke was the best thing to happen to him. Right now, she was the only person he considered a friend. The only one he trusted. She was his girl. His alone. He just needed to make sure she knew it. And soon. The rest he'd figure out later.

Chase kissed her hand, reassuring her again. "Forget what I said, okay? None of that crap matters because I'm not giving you up."

"But—"

He shook his head. "We're good, angel. Trust me, we're good."

Larke sighed, then rose from the bed. "All right. I'm trusting you, Chase." She moved across the room and opened up a drawer. "All I need now is for you to turn your back while I change."

He arched a brow. "How's that fair if you get to see me without a shirt but I don't get to see you?"

She laughed while pulling out a spaghetti strap shirt and shorts.

"I never said I was against double standards. I'm messing with you, though. I'll change inside the bathroom. Need to brush my teeth before bed like a good girl. You can help yourself to a toothbrush in the mirror cabinet. Any other man stuff you need, you're on your own." She tossed him a grin over her shoulder before closing the door behind her.

Minutes later when she came out of the bathroom, her braids had been done into two long twists that sort of resembled a French braid, hanging down the top of her back. His blood roared at the sight of her large breasts straining against the thin undershirt. His eyes lowered to the matching shorts that clung to her firm, plump ass. He ran a hand alongside his jaw and drew in a deep breath. *Driving me insane.*

Tearing his gaze from her and needing to calm himself, Chase entered the bathroom. After he returned to the bedroom, he was relieved to see Larke had changed her mind about sleeping in the living room. She was lying in bed, wrapped up in her floral comforter. On 'his' side of the bed, she'd left a blue and white checkered blanket. Same bed, separate sheets. Small favors, right? At least he wouldn't have to spend the night being tortured by having her body pressed against his, Chase thought while removing his pants and slipping into the bed beside her. She turned to him as the bed dipped beneath his frame and whispered, "I'm happy you stayed."

He stroked her face. "Did you ask me to stay because of what I told you happened to my father when we were kids?"

"That was my reason at first. I really was worried about you being tired. But then I thought about it and realized I really wanted you to stay here with me. Just because."

Chapter Eight

The next day Chase parked his truck in the driveway of the Antebellum Resistance meeting house-slash-headquarters and hopped out. As always, his stepfather was someone he tolerated because one, he was used to the man's behavior and two, because he had no other choice right now. If Chase had his way, he'd still be across town with his girl instead of having cigarette smoke blown his way.

And of course, in the blink of an eye, his mind was redirected to thoughts of Larke. He hoped she'd found the note he'd left for her this morning. He'd only been away from her for a couple of hours and already he was wishing to be next to her again.

Sometime during the middle of the night, Larke had rolled to the side of the bed he'd slept on. He'd known she was still fast asleep and had no idea what she was doing. If she had…

Drawing in a harsh breath, Chase turned the knob on the door to AR's main office, while recalling the way Larke had flung her thigh across him, nearly straddling his hips. If any other female had done that while in bed with him, he would've taken it as an invitation to thrust his dick so deep inside, giving them both what they wanted. At least the females he knew would've wanted it that way, and even expected it of him. Fast and hard. No drawn-out lovemaking.

As for Larke being so close to him... The only thing Chase had been able to do was to lie there, damn near breaking out in a sweat restraining himself. To get rid of his raging erection, he'd forced himself to think about so many things. All sorts of fucked up images—anything to make his cock soften before she awoke and realized how sick he was; wanting to fuck her while she slept. He'd even gone so far as to think about that damn reporter he'd witnessed his grandfather kill in cold blood. The sound of Trevor's laughter as the body hit the floor. *"That ain't a sound you hear every day, son."*

That memory, twisted at it was, had relieved him of any desire for sex. Thoughts of Larke, the things he'd heard and witnessed from childhood until now, coupled with everyone's expectations of him, caused Chase to lie in bed with his arm around her soft waist, seeking calm from the one person who could give it.

When morning arrived and Larke was fast asleep, he'd forced himself to climb out of the bed, however. He hadn't wanted to crowd her space or make her feel awkward in the morning with him still there.

On the way inside the building, Chase muttered a curse as he caught sight of McNair talking to John Delway, another member he'd grown up with. The two men grew quiet as he walked by. Chase narrowed his gaze at McNair, still pissed about the incident in the bar. Didn't matter if his thinking was hypocritical and unfair, or that the two of them had been raised with the same teachings.

"Hey Hudson," McNair called out, after catching up to him. "I saw you turn onto Glencove Boulevard last night. What's up, man? Did you go over to the dark side to start some shit?"

Delway snickered beside them at the idea of Chase visiting the predominately black and Hispanic area. Of course, the idiot would find it funny. His father thought all sorts of crime was funny and was, in fact, serving a fifteen-year prison term for robbing a convenience store and beating the Muslim owner.

Chase cocked his head and grinned. He'd seen McNair's car not too far behind his as he'd turned off in the direction of Larke's apartment building. Chase thought about asking the man if he'd been on a late run to Spicy n' Fine Taco Restaurant, where he'd seen McNair's car parked a couple of weeks ago. He thought better of it, for now. Wasn't like the asshole would admit to it anyway.

"Awe," Chase groaned, planting a look of exaggerated sympathy on his face. "Were you up all night crying cause I made you feel left out? Did you wanna tag along?"

"Hmm. Funny, man. Real funny."

Chase stared at him, smirking as McNair's finger scratched the bump on his off-centered nose, snorted then walked away. Chase watched him go. The man was all talk, and Chase had proven that after their one and only encounter as teenagers. McNair had cracked jokes and taunted him in front of others, doling out reasons why his mother had taken off, leaving him behind. Before McNair knew what had hit him, Chase had him pinned to the ground, pummeling his face until the other teen was screaming with a broken nose and bleeding all over the ground. It had taken two older AR members to tear Chase off him.

He continued down the hallway inside the building and entered Trevor's office. The stench of cigarette smoke hit his nostrils. Typical. Although it had only been a week since he last saw his stepfather, Chase was shocked to see the older man's thinner appearance. He hadn't lost a ton of weight but the few pounds he'd lost was very noticeable. His hair, which was slicked back into a long ponytail, seemed lankier than usual. Chase shrugged. It was anyone's guess what Trevor was smoking, snorting or even injecting in addition to his nicotine addiction.

"Just the man I wanted to see," Trevor said, swiveling side to side in his chair. "Everything went fine like I said it would?"

"Yep," Chase answered. The trip to Jacksonville had gone

uneventful, as well as getting the liquor into the right hands on the ship. *Last time.* Chase gritted his teeth while eyeing the older man. "So, what's up? I'm guessing you didn't want to meet with me to talk about the trip."

Trevor laughed, the sound came out as ugly as a knife scraping against glass. "Right you are. We need to talk business. But first…" Trevor popped open a new package of cigarette. "Want one?"

Chase shook his head. "Nope. You keep offering, but nothing's change. I don't smoke."

"Sorry." Trevor let out a breath. "I tell you what. You're right not to smoke this shit. It kills. Trust me."

Chase raised his brows. Was he trying to tell him something important? Maybe the sudden weight loss, the cough that sounded like he was about to vomit up a lung were signs of illness. Chase gave a mental shrug. "You okay?"

"Truth?" Trevor blew smoke out the side of his mouth. He kicked one leg up on the table. "I'm dying. Docs are telling me I only have a couple of months left." He snorted and chuckled low. "What the fuck do they know, right?"

Chase stared blankly at the only man he'd known as a father. He'd never felt love for Trevor and doubted his stepdad felt any for him. But damn, he should feel something. Sadness. Pity. This was a person he'd known since he was three years old. Chase gave himself a few seconds to muster up emotion. Nothing. He forced a note of concern into his voice. "Is it cancer?"

Trevor nodded. "Lungs are covered with tumors."

"What about chemo?" Chase asked, with genuine interest.

"Won't help. I already asked. Cancer's spread too far." Trevor ground the butt of the cigarette in the ashtray. "We're soldiers, right? Coming from a long line of genetically superior beings. I'm just a number, man. One of many. I ain't afraid of death so long as I know what we're doing here will continue—making the good ol' U.S of A as it should be. Like our ancestors wanted it to be before those yanks stuck their noses in where it never belonged. I'm heading to Heaven, boy. That sweet afterlife, reserved for our kind. Nothing tainted by goddamn Jews and their liberal multicultural media brainwashing. No siree. Ain't no place in Heaven for—"

Chase growled in frustration, cutting off Trevor's rant. "And while you're in this non-Jew Heaven, what about AR? What happens now?"

"New leadership. I'm looking at it, ain't I? Your great gramps was a direct descendant of one of the bravest soldiers that fought for the Confederacy. Your granddad Joe used his own money to buy up most of this land after that coal mine went out of business. He provided a place for those of us brave enough to step away from all the bullshit media telling us being around coloreds and immigrants is a good thing. That it's cool. Fuck no. We both know I was always just a filler. It's your time to step up, Chase. I know you're loyal to seeing our people take control once again. That's why we need you to take the helm and lead. Show those motherfuckers out there what real nationalism is about."

Chase knew this was coming. Hell, hadn't he been waiting on this for years? He schooled his features, not sure how to react. The only word his mind could form was *Larke*. How loyal was he, if hours ago he'd been in bed with a girl who was everything he was supposed to hate?

Trevor spoke of legacy, heritage, and loyalty. But Chase felt divided. The loyalty he once thought was hundred percent centered on his racist beliefs, was now leaning toward the vision of brown beauty, who had curled up against him last night. Smiling.

Her lips full and juicy, reflecting a heritage he should revile, had whispered in his ear, caressed his skin. Tenderly kissing his symbols of hate as if they were bruises. Horrible bruises she wanted to help him heal. Chase pinched his forehead and asked, "When do you want to exchange leadership?"

Trevor shrugged. "Well, it ain't like I'm keeling over tonight. We got some time to sort it all out. Not like I gotta worry about you not stepping up."

Chase nodded. He also understood everything Trevor said and didn't say. Him stepping up or taking over as leader of AR wasn't really a choice. It was pretty much a guarantee, because as he and every other kid who grew up in Lee's Fortress understood–Antebellum Resistance was bigger than them. This was about securing the right future. Their personal goals and feelings didn't count for shit.

Trevor lit up another cigarette and leaned back in his chair. Chase groaned silently as his stepdad regarded him with a smirk while shaking his head. He knew what was coming. And not surprisingly, the older man switched to his favorite topic. Women.

"You still ain't got yourself a girl?" Trevor asked this question every couple of weeks. "I ain't talking 'bout some random bitch to screw. A proper girl. You know, the kind you wanna settle down with. Knock up and start having some young'uns."

Chase chuckled despite his annoyance. If Trevor knew the kind of girl he was thinking about fucking all the time, the man would drop dead from a heart attack long before cancer took him out. He shook his head and relaxed in his chair. "Nope. I damn sure ain't in a rush to attach myself to one girl, much less be anyone's daddy."

Trevor grunted. "Meh, you ain't too wrong there. Sometimes kids turn out to be the biggest disappointment. Take the son I had before I met your no-good mother. Biggest piece of shit ever." He lit up another cigarette and propped one elbow on the table, his eyes gleaming with amusement. "I tell you what. Couple of years ago–you were just a kid then–I got a letter from my…" He made air quotes. "Son. Brainwashed garbage is what he is. Begging me to renounce my *racist* ways and come out to California to meet him and his Jap wife. Pathetic fool even got her pregnant. Wanted me to meet his little mongrels." He made a sound of disgust. "Can you believe that shit?"

Chase curled his lips and said what he knew the man expected to hear. What any white supremacist would say to another who was dealing with race mixing within their own family. "Sorry you had to deal with that, man. Must have been real tough." He knew it wasn't much of a response, but damn. It was the best he could muster.

Trevor nodded, obviously pleased with Chase's response. "That's life. At least I got one son who won't pull some race mixing shit like that. Your gramps and I raised you with sense."

Chase had stopped listening. All he could focus on was getting away. Far from Lee's Fortress, where he didn't have to see Trevor's face or hear his hacking cough ever again. But that wouldn't happen. The only refuge he had was the small house he'd bought a year ago, over an hour's drive away.

Sitting upright, Chase cleared his throat, suddenly bolstered by the thought of leaving. "Listen. I'm gonna be out of town for a couple of days. Don't bother to call my phone or email me. I'm not checking any of that stuff. Need some days to relax."

Trevor chuckled and held up his hand. "You're going away with a bitch. Yeah. Yeah. I got it. You won't hear me calling. Said what I had to, anyway. We're done here."

Chase nodded. One thing was to be said for Trevor. The man was good at reading between the lines and despised awkward small talk as much as he did. Chase stood. He made it halfway out the door when Trevor called out. "Hey, Chase. Remember what I said. Stop messing around with them sluts and get yourself a good woman. A real dedicated female with enough pride who'll give you what you need."

Chase tightened his fist around the handle of the door, fighting the urge to rip it off and shove it down Trevor's corroding throat. Grinding his teeth, he said nothing, only issuing a single, curt nod. Now his dick was expected to be on AR duty, breeding precious white babies.

He powered down the hallway and out of the building. Life was a teasing bitch. If he wasn't so frustrated, he would've laughed;

because the sad thing was, a month ago he would've given serious thought to Trevor's words.

Seated inside his truck, Chase clasped his hands together. He struggled to maintain his calm. *Always so much damn pressure.* He drew in a deep breath and reached for his phone. There was a missed call from Larke, followed by a message.

Saw your note. No prob. Hope I didn't hog the bed last night!

The tension began to drain from his body. Chase smiled. His conversation with Trevor was now a distant memory. *You did,* he wrote back. *But I liked it. Can I call u?*

Not now. I have a friend over.

Who?

Why do you want to know?

Chase stared at the phone. His smile vanished. Was Larke teasing him or was she serious? He'd never made a habit of texting anyone unless it was something real important.

He didn't get the chance to reply, before another message came through. *Chase. Are you scowling?*

He was. She knew him. *I was joking with you. I'm sorry if it didn't come across well.* She inserted a smiley face at the end of her apology.

Good. But he still wanted to know who she was with. Anger crept into him. It had better not be that asshole who he'd seen her with inside the bowling alley. The one who'd slapped her ass. His scowl deepened as he asked again. *Who's with u?*

Riva. My only friend. Apart from you. But Chase are you still scowling?

Relief made him grin. *Yeah. Real nasty too. You wouldn't wanna see it.*

I knew it! Forgive me?

Maybe.

Maybe? I want you to say yes.

Okay. Yes. Only if you let me see you again today.

Of course. I want to see you too.

His chest felt tight again. *Where?*

Same park. In an hour. Near the duck pond.

Chase held the phone inside his hand. Two things suddenly occurred to him. He'd actually texted a girl and could've continued doing so if they hadn't just agreed to meet. *And,* he was still parked outside the main building, smiling like he'd won the lottery.

Chapter Nine

"I can't believe you're rushing me out."

"I'm not," Larke lied. "I'm only telling you I have to go." Riva gave her a sideways glance and slanted her lips. "Well, yeah I see that. But why did you go to the bathroom and put on makeup?"

"It's only eye makeup. Not even a lot." She hoped it wasn't too much.

"Aha. So, you admit it. Who is he? I know it's not Kevin because I saw him the other day and he was confused as to why you didn't want a second date."

Oh, Lord. Larke rolled her eyes. "Seriously? Did he think I liked having him grope me inside a bowling alley?"

Riva shrugged. "I told him that. Whatever. Forget Kevin. When I came back from the bathroom I caught you grinning and texting. Tell me who it is. Another writer? Where'd you meet him and why are you being so secretive?"

She dabbed her lips with lip gloss and laughed. Riva was fishing for info. But Larke was smarter than that, she wasn't going to slip and talk about Chase. Her friend wouldn't understand. No one would. To be honest she didn't even want to try and explain her feelings for Chase to anyone only to be judged and told she was insane.

"You're imagining things. I was messaging my dad. He has a new phone and was trying out some of the messaging features. Just being silly." The worst lie in the history of lies.

"Liar," Riva muttered. "I'll let you off this time. I get it. Anyways. We'll catch up soon and then you're gonna tell me all about this mystery man." She grabbed up her handbag and threw Larke a teasing glance from the doorway. "Have fun and I hope he's good looking."

"Thanks," Larke said, trying hard to contain the excitement bubbling inside her.

On the way to the park, her skin tingled and the butterflies inside her stomach did somersaults each time she thought about last night. Chase's kisses. She could still feel his mouth on hers, hot, scorching her with the intensity of his lips. How she'd nervously climbed into the bed, fully aware he would join her.

First time being so close to a man. That had been awkward, but oh so wonderful once he'd lain beside her and stroked her face. Somewhere deep inside, Larke knew she should feel guilty and bad for allowing Chase into her heart. She couldn't. No one was perfect, and he was *not* a horrible person.

Last night, after seeing the way he'd hung his head after questioning him about his beliefs, Larke knew any sane person would say he deserved the shame he obviously felt. Still, it wasn't something she'd taken pleasure in witnessing. Not at all. If anything, his behavior had further proven to her that he was no beast. Beneath the hardened exterior and hate, was a person with real feelings and emotions that went far beyond race. That was something she couldn't and would not ignore.

Once she'd reached the park and found a spot near the pond, Larke exited her car. She smoothed her skirt, gave her braids a quick pat although they were held back in a brightly colored wrap, tied from the back to the front with an off-centered bow. By the time she arrived at the pond, her entire body was rippling with anticipation. Chase had made it there before her and was seated with his bare arms stretched across the back of a bench. Larke glanced around making sure there weren't too many people. She didn't wish for anyone to feel uncomfortable. Thankfully, they were alone.

Her cheeks heated the moment he looked her way and rose to greet her. She drew in a deep breath, battling the mounting urgency to squeeze her legs together and quell the pulsating need building between her thighs.

"Hey." His voice, deep and gruff made her breath catch.

"You beat me here."

"Thought I'd impress you by showing up early."

Larke laughed softly, drawn in by the way his blue eyes appeared more vivid than before. "You impress me. But not because you arrived here before me." She settled next to him. "You said in your note that you had to meet with someone this morning. Did it go well?"

"Yeah, it was my stepfather." He gazed at her and rubbed the bottom of his chin. "I found out he's dying of cancer. Only has a couple of months to live."

Larke searched her mind for the right thing to say. What did one say to the news that a horrible racist was dying? She sighed. Racist bastard or not, he probably meant something to Chase, so she forced herself to say, "I'm sorry. Is he suffering a lot?"

Chase chuckled without humor. "He's got lung cancer and still smoking like five packs a day. It's sick."

The lack of emotion in his voice confused her. "Won't you miss your stepfather when he dies? I remember you mentioned him to me when we were kids."

His eyes went cold. "When you clip a fingernail, do you ever miss it? I mean it was a part of you for a while, right?"

Ouch. Larke kept her tone neutral. "Isn't this different? He's a human being. He helped raised you, didn't he?"

"Yeah, that's true. But your thinking is wrong. He didn't raise me out of the goodness of his heart after my mother left. Trevor was all about getting in good with my grandfather. He practically moved right in after my father died when I was three. He used my mother to get himself lined up in a good position to take over when my grandfather couldn't handle the work anymore. Trevor wanted and needed my loyalty as I got older. Nothing more, nothing less."

"*Does* he have your loyalty?"

Chase shrugged. "To an extent. Just how it is. We've got our ways and the rest of the world have theirs."

"Have you ever thought about leaving? I mean, turning your..." Larke stopped in mid-sentence at the expression on his face. The one telling her she was pushing a subject he didn't want or wasn't ready to confront.

"We're on the wrong topic."

"Then what topic *do* you want to discuss?"

He eyes glinted like shards of ice. Warning. A tense second passed before he said, "I wanted you to know that I'm going up to Lake Walnut for a couple of days."

A couple of days without seeing him. She tried not to feel sad. After all, he *was* about to get angry with her just a minute ago. "Are you going alone?"

"Depends." He shifted on the bench, lowered his gaze then leveled up to face her.

Larke frowned. She recognized that look. Chase was nervous. But why? "What does it depend on?"

"Depends on if you wanna come with me or not. It's a small house I have up there. It ain't fancy. Real clean, though. Has two bedrooms, so you wouldn't have to worry about sharing a room with me. If you like this park, you'll love the woods and lakes they have up there." He lifted a shoulder. "But if you're not into that sort of thing, it's cool. I'll understand."

"I'm into that sort of thing," she said, sweeping her fingers across his.

Chase's lips thinned into a faint smile as the traces of nervousness vanished. Once again, he appeared to be in control. Or rather, a man trying his best to appear in control. He nodded. "Okay. That's good. How much time do you need to be ready?"

She gaped. "You want to leave today?"

"Yeah, is that a problem?"

Not really, except I don't make a habit of running off with a guy on short notice. Larke groaned inside her head. What was she saying? They'd slept in the same bed last night! "No," she answered, "it's not a problem. I want to go, but I have my first book reading at a library coming up. If you promise to get me home by Tuesday afternoon, then I'll say yes."

"I'll have you back by then."

She nodded, biting back a smile at his immediate reassurance. "If you give me an hour I can be packed and ready. Is it chilly up there? Do I need a sweater or three?"

He stared at her then laughed. The sound was a delicious rumble that made her stomach do a backflip. "Larke, don't tell me you bring sweaters wherever you go? Even in the middle of summer."

She poked him in the arm. "You laugh now, but it was my sweater that kept both our butts from freezing."

He shook his head, the smile still in place. "I never did thank you for that, did I? Sharing your sweater and candy with me."

"You planned on thanking me?" She sucked in an exaggerated breath of shock and flattened her hand to her chest. "And to think all these years I'd assumed you not using that knife on me was your way of saying thanks."

His smiled faded. "Did you really think that?"

"No," Larke said. "But sometimes I think about that day. What would've happened if we hadn't fallen inside the sinkhole. You had a pretty good hold on my shirt. I was very scared and didn't understand why you were after me. I hadn't done anything to you."

"I know," he whispered, so low she could barely hear him. "I know you hadn't done anything to me."

Larke recognized the meaning of the way his shoulders bunched. Guilt. She grabbed a hold of that emotion and decided to use it as a way to peek inside his mind. If Chase felt guilt for his treatment of her, then perhaps he had remorse and this, in turn, could lead him to reevaluate his racist views.

"Do you think you would've hurt me? Looking back, would you have used that knife on me? You were so young. Did you really have it inside of you to do that?"

He slanted his head to the side. Larke could see a muscle in his jaw tick. "What is this—you trying to psychoanalyze me?"

She shrugged. "Maybe. You can psychoanalyze me later. I'm not perfect. I have issues too. All I want is for you to look me in the eyes and tell me if you could've killed me because of my skin color."

He glared at her, his eyes murky like a storm cloud. "This ain't my answer; but what happens if I say yes? I feel like you're trying to mess with me, fuck with my head to get back at me for…" He closed his mouth and shook his head. Seconds passed before he let out a loud breath of anger and frustration. Her heart twisted, realizing he had a *lot* of frustration. It was always there, despite his ensuing words of, "Nothing. Just nothing."

She touched his arm while peering up at him. "I want to know what's going on in your head. It's never *nothing*. Why do you think I'd want to get back at you? I don't. It's been too many years. And what would I get back at you for, Chase? For being what you are? For being you?"

He nodded ever so slowly, looking her dead in the eyes. "For being me. Definitely for being me."

"I'd never treat you like that."

"Then why do you need to know what I would've done when I was eleven? What difference does it make?"

"It makes a difference because I want to know what I'm up against. If I didn't care about you, I wouldn't have agreed to go away with you or invite you into my apartment for the night. This caring might also develop into something deeper." She let out a breath. "I see so much in you beyond the white supremacy and secrecy. If you tell me you couldn't have gone through with hurting me, then I'll know the hate isn't as deep inside you as you think it is. However, if you say you could have, *would* have hurt me that violently, then I'll definitely know what I believe about you is true."

"That I'm a dirty racist fucker?"

"No." Larke flattened her hand against his chest. "That's not what I meant at all. You told me I didn't have any reason to be afraid of you and I believe you with all my heart. That's why I have hope. Because it shows me how far you've come and how far I believe you want to go, even if you're not ready to admit or accept it. I'll always have hope, no matter what you say."

"I would've tried," he admitted slowly, covering her hand with his. "But I wouldn't have gone through with it. A month before I saw you near the woods, I'd witnessed something. Shit, no kid should ever have to see. I'm not trying to use it as an excuse, but I need you to understand that my mind was more messed up than it usually was. Seeing you on our property triggered a lot of my anger. I fucked up a hundred percent. I'm sorry. Also for any names I called you. I'm really sorry."

Larke nodded. Her eyes stung with tears. She blinked them back. "Do you want to talk about what you saw?"

He shook his head and his Adam's apple bobbed. "I shouldn't have mentioned it. What's important is that you know you're safe with me. Always."

Her eyes stung some more. Chase was trying. He really was. She could already see a change in him from the crude person who'd had her fearing for her safety weeks ago. "I know I'm safe with you. And you're safe with me too. I won't ever hurt you."

He eyed her up and down. For a second she worried he would point out the obvious difference in their size, blowing off the true meaning of her words. He didn't. Chase closed his arm around her shoulder and drew her close. He slanted his lips above hers then said, "We're good together, Larke."

She smiled while trying to steady her erratic breathing. "We'll be better when you tell me what to do about my sweaters. I can't be cold."

He groaned, nipping her ear. "Just one. But you won't need it with me close by. That I can promise you."

Chapter Ten

"You, uh, packed a lot," Chase said, minutes after they'd arrived inside the house surrounded by forest and lake. He glanced at his single duffle bag, dwarfed between Larke's two travel bags. He'd never gone away with a girl before, so he'd kept his mouth shut as he'd placed her bags in the backseat of his truck. Chase figured it must be normal. But damn, she'd even brought along a backpack that was bulging at the sides.

"I know it seems like a bit much." She studied her hands. "I like being prepared. That's all."

"Prepared for what, Larke? There's not much out here, except the woods and that big lake outside the window." Chase stared at her in confusion. She wasn't nuts. Not like some of the guys back at Lee's Fortress. Preppers—some real crazy sons of bitches, who'd started preparing by stockpiling all sorts of things for the race war that Chase now realized had always been a pipe dream. This was also the same war that was supposed to happen after the number of white supremacists grew strong enough for them to take control of the government and enact laws that would once and for all put all blacks and non-whites in their place.

Larke shrugged, still not quite meeting his eyes. "It's not a big deal. I don't like worrying that I don't have something I need when I'm away from home."

"So it's not just clothes and shoes you have in there? The usual female stuff." He watched her closely. She was nibbling her lower lip now, looking nervous. Trapped.

"I didn't think you'd be interested in what I brought along."

"I'm not," he answered. "I was teasing you before, But not anymore. Now I really wanna know what's going on." He cupped her chin, forcing her to meet his gaze. This had to be what she'd meant about having her own issues. "You think something bad's gonna happen to you if you're not somewhere familiar? Is that why you need to be prepared?"

She peered at him and nodded slowly. Chase closed his eyes then opened them on a low sigh. Damn. He'd hit the nail on the head despite praying he would miss. "Something bad like having to sleep out in the cold." *Because of me.*

"Oh, Chase. I feel so stupid. I'm not crippled by it, but I really dislike going anywhere new if I don't have certain things with me. Things that I might need. After we were rescued and I went home, I thought I was doing fine. I mean we were okay, no injuries. I'm not sure when exactly this began or what triggered this fear, but one day it hit me. I'd made one little mistake, got lost and could've died. I became terrified, completely scared to go anywhere new. My mom had to rearrange her shift and make arrangements for me to get home from school if she couldn't pick me up."

"How did you manage?" Guilt made it hard to speak.

"I stayed inside a lot. I never made many friends. The other kids thought I was weird." She lowered her lashes. "And well, I was fat, which didn't make things easier." Heaving a sigh, she continued, "Things changed as I got older. I wanted so much to do everything the other kids were doing. You know, school trips and hanging out. I later figured out that maybe all I needed was to be prepared for anything bad that was coming my way. I started bringing little things that might be helpful if I ever found myself in a sticky situation, in unfamiliar territory. It made me feel in control. Not so afraid." She issued him a weak smile. "I know all of this sounds really crazy. But it's the only weird thing about me. I promise."

"So that backpack over there is filled with survival gear?"

Larke bit her lip and nodded. "A low key, low budget version. Some basic items. Backup battery for my phone, first aid kit." Her lips thinned into another weak smile. "No candy, but I do have a couple of protein bars and a small blanket." The smile faded once again as she lowered her head. "I'm working on this too. I really don't want to always be scared. I don't like the feeling of anticipating the worst."

And with those words, Chase felt like absolute shit. It was bad enough she'd had to deal with what he'd put her through that evening in the woods, but to spend so many years afterward, being afraid... He drew in a breath and brought a hand to his mouth. He was sicker than he'd ever imagined.

He eyed her again then shifted his gaze to the bag. "You mind if I peek inside?"

"Go ahead." She knelt in front of the backpack while Chase crouched, slowly opening it. There was a flashlight inside, medical and antiseptic creams, a pocket knife, a thin rolled up blanket, a bunch of protein bars and four bottles of water.

Chase zipped the bag and turned to her. He'd seen enough. His gut clenched to see Larke peering at him with worry as if he had a right to judge her. He didn't. "That's a lot of stuff for one person," he pointed out.

"I know. I'm strange. I already told you."

He couldn't take his eyes off her. "There's nothing strange about you, Larke. Except you being with me—which works to my advantage," he added with a grin, hoping to make her smile. She did. Even pressed her face into his neck. He held her there, enjoying the feel of her soft body against his and the delicious scent of her skin. Chase cradled the back of her head, forcing her to meet his gaze. "You packed for both of us, didn't you, angel?"

She sank a tooth into her lip and nodded. His hand at the back of her head stilled. It felt as if someone had suctioned all the air from the living room. Or maybe just from his lungs; because breathing suddenly became one of his hardest tasks. On the floor and staring into her dark glossy eyes, Chase thought about everything she'd said. Everything he'd done to mess up her thinking when it came to new surroundings. And yet, in Larke's wacky way of planning, she'd still included his no-good ass.

Invisible strings tugged at his heart, pushing him mentally and physically closer to her. She leaned over with her hands planted on the floor. Her lips parted, welcoming his tongue against her own. His cock hardened and his balls felt as if they weighed a ton, heavy with cum.

God. Chase closed his palm over her breast, kneading and caressing. One move and he knew he could have her on her back, right here on the hard living room floor. But would she let him in?

Control. He struggled with it and was relieved when Larke used her own, taking the reins by tearing her lips from his. She moaned softly, her breathing shallow as she gazed up at him with big brown eyes.

"There's no going back is there?"

He swallowed hard. "None at all."

They both stood, uncaring that they'd barely made it into the living room without touching each other. "I told you before that I'd never physically been with anyone before," Larke said, "But it's more than that. I've never had an actual relationship either. This is my first and I'm actually very happy it's with you. Sometimes I've even wondered if we were meant to meet up again." She smiled shyly. "Whenever I think about you or being your girl, I get these butterflies that flutter like crazy inside my stomach." Her smile widened as she let out a quiet laugh. "Which is a *good* thing. Not a sign of my craziness."

She cleared her throat and her voice went low as she peered up at him. "Anyway, since you now know almost everything about me. That you're the only man in my life, how can I be sure there's not some blue-eyed, blonde 'Aryan' dream girl, waiting for you to get back home?"

The question stung. But it was fair. Just like how it was also fair that those damn butterflies she'd mentioned had now found their way inside his stomach as well. "There's no one," Chase answered. "I swear it. That girl you described isn't the type of girl I want. Not anymore. I'm one man, Larke. I only need one woman at my side and that's you. I want you more than any other female I've ever met. I'm no virgin, but I can tell you I've never had a girl of my own before. So yeah, I guess we have that in common. You're my first girlfriend."

Her eyes widened then a bright smile broke out on her face. "Honestly?"

His cheeks burned hotter than the sun outside at her grin of pure happiness. "Yeah, honestly." Chase cleared his throat with a fake cough then averted his attention to the bags still resting near the doorway. "Anyway. Forget what I said about your bags, there's nothing wrong with being prepared. Shit happens all the time, right?"

"Yes it does," she agreed. "And we'll be ready for it."

He'd have to be ready for it, Chase thought. If anyone he knew realized who Larke was, what she meant to him… There were just too many well-meaning idiots in their neo-Confederate movement who might think they were doing him a favor.

Schooling his concerns, Chase slapped a smile on his lips. It wasn't entirely fake because being near Larke, in general, made him feel relaxed.

"Is this your home away from home?" She was staring out of a large window overlooking the lake. "Do you come here often?"

Chase joined her, holding the curtain away from the glass. "It's supposed to be. I bought it last year. Only been here like twice, though. There's a lot of hunting ground. Not like over at Lee's Fortress. Most of the woodland was cut down to make room for new houses.

She turned to him, an almost horrified and hurt expression on her face. He wished he'd kept his mouth close. "You guys have a lot of members, don't you?"

"We have enough." He silently cursed himself for putting that look on her face. He schooled his features again, refusing to give her the details she obviously wanted. Details that would only cause more pain. "I got this place to get away and do some proper hunting."

Not wanting her mind to stay focused on his earlier comment, Chase led her from the window and showed her the rest of the house. The two bedrooms, each with its own bathroom and the patio the woodlands. When Larke sighed and mentioned how much she'd love to live somewhere out in the middle of nature, his chest hurt.

She was a lot like himself. Her words reminded him once again, how so many of the things he'd been told about people different from himself didn't add up. After he'd shown her the entire house, Chase threw on a long-sleeved shirt before heading to the supermarket with Larke. Another first. Grocery shopping with a girl. His girl.

"Those are interesting ingredients," she said, as he placed bottles of spices into the shopping cart. Most of them he'd never heard of or used before. He glanced at his phone, double-checking the ingredient list.

"I know." He pretended to ignore her curiosity. "I'm not telling you what I'm going to cook. You can quit fishing for info."

She let out an exaggerated sigh of annoyance. As they strolled down the aisle it was hard not to notice all the people around them. Couples walking together and talking. Like him and Larke. It all seemed so normal. Here, it was okay for them to pretend normalcy.

He was a regular guy out with his girl. Sure, there were a few stares, which probably came because they seemed so mismatched. With him looking like a mean son of a bitch and Larke so damn sweet and friendly. But still, this was a feeling he wished they could have all the time. The two of them, no race bullshit in between. No pressure of fulfilling a role or having people he was starting to care less and less about, depend on him to lead them into a future he was beginning to despise.

Back at the house, Chase's nerves started to screw with him. Not because he was alone with her again. That he loved. His nerves were going insane because of guilt. His need to show her how sorry he was. Pay Larke back for everything she'd done for him. Asking him to stay at her place the other night because she remembered something he'd told her so long ago and cared. Thinking about him all the time, in ways no one else had ever done.

Chase shook his head. *And she's supposed to be the enemy. Everything wrong with this country. Sub-human.* "Fucking bullshit."

"Putting the drinks in the freezer's bullshit?"

Chase blinked, realizing he'd spoken out loud. Larke was standing by the refrigerator holding two plastic bottles in her hand and gaping at him.

"No," he said. He tried to recall what she'd said to him but drew a blank. "Did you say something?"

"I wanted to know which drink I should put in the freezer so it gets cold really fast. Cola or the fruit punch?"

"Both. They'll fit."

She popped the bottles in to cool then turned to face him, her eyes filled with concern. "You zoned out, didn't you? Is it anything you want to talk about?"

"Not now," he murmured. Chase closed his arms around her, desperate for the feel of her touch, like an anchor grounding him to the only reality he wanted. And she understood! Larke laid her head against his chest until the angry thoughts and frustration retreated into the darkest corners of his mind. That was the placed he hid all thoughts that had nothing to do with the here and now. Like his future with her. That took up the largest part of his mental hideaway, which he was closing off for the night. Nothing but the here and now with his girl for as long as they stayed tucked away by the lake.

Holding her at arm's length, he smiled. "All right. Go catch up on your book. Relax. Do whatever, as long as you stay out of the kitchen until I tell you to come."

"Or until the fire alarm goes off?" Her lips twitched.

He narrowed his eyes, pretending anger. "You doubting me?"

"As a matter of fact, yes!" Larke placed a hand on her hip. "I'm a little worried since you were looking at some of those spices, reading off the names like it was a foreign language or something."

"Real funny. All right, tell me when was the last time you cooked with cardamom, or whatever it's called."

"Last week," she shot back. Her lips twitched even more. "I'm lying. You're right. I'll leave you to cook while I watch something on my laptop in the bedroom." Halfway across the room, she glanced over her shoulder. Her eyes twinkled playfully as she said, "If that alarm goes off, I'm grabbing my bag and your hand then we're getting the hell out of here, okay?"

"First alarm is a warning the food might be burnt. Second one, you can grab the bag."

She laughed. "Deal."

Chapter Eleven

Larke chewed on and swallowed her statement from earlier. Chase was actually a wonderful cook, which was surprising for a man who appeared so out of place inside a kitchen. Even though the alarm went off once, she'd yet to see or taste a burnt morsel of the cardamom and maple flavored salmon.

The man seated across from her at the table was like an enigma wrapped in a puzzle then thrown into the middle of a maze. She was stuck right there inside with him. The two of them. And she wouldn't have it any other way.

Larke watched as Chase stood and began clearing away the dishes, which she'd planned on doing. She pushed out of her chair, reached for a glass but couldn't get her hand around it. He placed his hand atop hers, swiping the glass and thwarting her move.

"I'll do it," he said abruptly. "You can relax."

She brushed his hand away. "I relaxed while you were cooking. Now you sit back while I clean up." She grabbed the glass and jokingly said, "I need to burn off some calories from all the food, anyway."

"No, you don't. Now give it to me. I told you, I'm doing this." His tone was gruffer than usual, confusing her.

She kept her hand around the glass, slowly shaking her head. "And I told you I'm helping. Like you helped me in my apartment." She lowered her voice to offset the gruff tone he'd used with her. Larke disliked arguments. "That's how these things usually work."

Chase drew his head up, eyes flickering with ice. "I ain't a fucking kid. I know what helping is. You don't have to explain it to me."

She flinched. Hurt by his reaction. She released the glass, folded her arms around her middle and took a step backward. "I can clearly see you're not a child. That still doesn't explain why you don't want my help." She stared at him and bit her inner cheek as a horrible thought struck her. Did Chase have some kind of hang up about black people touching his stuff? In a way that would make sense, but... No. She'd done more than touch his belongings. She'd *used* them. And there was also the kissing, her hands and lips *touching* his hard body.

His low intake of breath told her he'd read the look on her face and knew what she was thinking, assuming. The glass in his hand hit the table without breaking. Shocked, Larke glanced upward to see him bearing down on her. "No," he grated, pointing a finger at her and shaking his head hard. "It is *nothing* like what you're thinking."

"What I'm thinking?"

"Yes," he shouted. "What you're goddamn thinking." His eyes narrowed to slits. "Larke, I see the look on your face. I know you're wondering if this is some kind of weird shit from me because you're..." He stopped in mid-sentence. Took another deep breath, stepped away then came right back until he was blocking her space. Her head bumped his chest.

"I don't want your help. I don't want you helping me because I don't deserve it. Now do you get it?"

Her eyes widened. The anger in his voice, anger directed at himself instead of her, nearly ripped her heart in two. Larke opened her mouth to reassure him that everything he'd said wasn't true, but couldn't. He was gazing at her, his eyes hazy as he spoke. So low she could barely hear him. But hear him she did. Every single word that made her heartbeat thunder.

"I'm really sorry for screwing with your head. Making you afraid to go out and not enjoy life as you should have when you were a kid. I'm sorry that because of me you think you have to always be prepared for being left out in the cold. And I'm sorry for coming to you with my fucked up thoughts and beliefs. I'm trying, Larke. I'm really trying to fix them. Just hope you can keep being patient with me, like you've been so far."

The pain reflected in his eyes tore into her. Her legs wobbled and her entire body felt shaky, witnessing the man she cared so much about consumed with regret and feelings laid bare. It was too much. Larke sank back onto the chair and covered her mouth with her hand, attempting to keep her tears at bay. It was useless. One droplet after the other dampened her cheek.

A harsh groan split from his throat. Chase knelt on the ground in front of her, sweeping his thumb against her cheek to wipe the tears. "Hey, come on. I didn't say that to make you cry."

She sniffled. "I know you didn't."

"I only wanted to show you how sorry I am. I didn't know what else to do. That's why I cooked. Thought you might find it special if I did the work instead of taking you out to eat somewhere."

"It was very special." She wrapped her arm around his neck, wetting his skin with leftover tears. "Thank you."

He flashed her a lopsided grin, causing her pulse to race. "I also didn't want you to lift a finger since this is all about me making it up to you."

Her blood warmed and her lower belly cinched. Chase's deep raspy tone was turning her insides to mush. His eyes gazing into hers as if he knew exactly the effect he was having on her, made her folds slicken with moisture. "Can I lift a finger to touch you?" she asked dazed with arousal.

Chase took her hand between his, stroking it against his lip. "That's allowed. But only me. You can only touch me."

Larke licked her lips, a heady mixture of fear and desire leading her thoughts. "How much touching are we talking about? The kind where we go off to separate rooms, or…" She never finished. Chase's hand was now gliding upward, beneath her dress, laying waste to any thoughts inside her head that didn't center on the decadent feel of his rough fingers on her skin.

Her heartbeat thumped against her chest, beating an arcane rhythm. Larke thanked God a thousand times over, that she was already seated, because surely her legs would've buckled and folded by now. Her breath hitched in the middle of her throat as his hand grazed higher, slipping inside her panties. His fierce gaze held her pinned.

The world around her seemed to stop until the moment she held her breath for finally happened. Chase's fingers on her pussy. Larke trembled and sucked in a deep breath. Heat flared to life, blazing inside her lower belly.

He caressed two digits between her moist labia. His low, ragged groan intertwined with the soft gasp tumbling from the back of her throat. "Angel, you're so wet for me." His eyes glinted with surprise. "I barely touched you."

"I can't help it," she whimpered. "I get very wet when I think about you." Another groan rumbled from his chest.

Chase fondled and rubbed his thumb over her engorged clitoris, which throbbed heavily when his lips tilted into an almost boyish grin. Pressing her back to the chair for support, Larke sank her teeth into her bottom lip the moment he delved the tip of his index finger inside her pussy.

"Feels really tight and warm." His lids lowered, fixed on her exposed sex.

She rolled her hips, undulating on the seat while vaguely registering him asking her, "Want more?"

Chase added another finger without waiting for her sharp cry of, "Yes. P–please." Larke whimpered and flinched at the invasion of his middle and index fingers pumping shallow strokes inside her. Over and over. With one hand cupping her waist, he held her firm, anchoring the ripples coursing through her body.

Lips parted, she ground her bottom against the seat, wanting— waiting for something that seemed so close. With every thrust of his fingers, her body tensed, beads of pleasure careening through and enveloping every inch of her body. Larke moaned, spreading her thighs wider. She was about to come. And nothing like the mini orgasms she'd felt while pleasuring herself in bed at night.

"Ohhh! Don't stop." She was begging, pleading while her hands gripped his massive shoulders for support.

"Wasn't planning to," Chase grated. "Wanna see you come all over my fingers."

It didn't take much else. Her entire body became undone, shuddering with waves of pleasure rippling down her spine, making her toes curl. Riding out the last of her orgasm Larke fluttered her lids open. She stroked his face with the back of her hand.

A slow smile worked its way across her lips. "That was incredible." Her body shivered again with remnants of ecstasy. "I made myself come sometimes but it was never as pleasurable. Not even close."

"I like hearing that," he said throatily, withdrawing his soaked fingers from between her labia. Her stomach flipped as he raised his head. There was a knowing smile on his face. Larke glanced down, her cheeks suddenly burning. Oh. She'd yet to close her legs. She tried to bring them together. Couldn't because Chase was holding them apart and shaking his head.

"Hey," he murmured in a hushed tone. "It's okay, Larke. I won't do anything. I only want to look at you spread real nice and wide for me." His eyes softened. "Thinking about my cock sliding into you. All that heat."

Oh my God. A moan escaped from her lips. Chase brought his head up, brows arched. "Why'd you moan?"

"Because of what you said." She tried to catch her breath. "It turned me on."

He squeezed her thigh. "Are you getting wet again because I want to shove my dick really hard in your pussy over and over. 'Till you can feel me all the way up near your belly." He pushed her panties aside again to check her. Larke held her breath, knowing he would find her shamefully drenched with arousal even though minutes ago she'd come all over his fingers.

"You know exactly what you're doing to me when you say those things. When you talk to me like that."

His lips curved into a crooked grin that made her clit pulsate and swell. "I do," he admitted quietly. "You're so wet. Dripping with need. Begging for a cock from the way I see it." His steel blue eyes grew dark. Fierce. "I think it's high time you had a man between those beautiful thighs." His smile faded as he brought her legs together, closing them. "Fact of the matter is, I'd like to be that man, Larke. I won't push you into anything you're not ready for. But you have to know, see how much I want you. If you're feeling the way I do right now and from the look on your face, I think you are; then all you have to do is let me know that you want this too." He brushed her cheek with his knuckle. "I'd be real gentle, with it being your first time and all. I know I don't look it, but I got a lot of self-control when I need it."

Oh Heaven. Was Chase pleading with her to let him be her first? Her heart thundered and her pussy clenched, throbbing like never before. There was no need to plead! She wanted, craved him inside her. Her body shivered with anticipation.

Recalling his order from earlier, Larke asked, "If I'm only allowed to touch you, does that mean you'll remove my clothes?"

He gazed at her then dropped his head to her lap, groaning loud. "Yes! I'll take off your clothes, do everything. Spread your legs myself as long as I get to fuck you."

She nodded despite his rough tone making her insides melt with desire. When Chase lifted her in his arms and strode across the house toward the bedroom, Larke tried to keep her composure, hard as it was. She could feel his rough fingers against her skin, teasing. He grasped the braids off her back, holding them to her head while dotting kisses to her nape. Cool air caressed her skin the second he unzipped her dress and skimmed the length of her back as the dress pooled at her feet.

He's serving me.

As much as it broke her heart that he felt the need to do this, Larke reveled in the new sensation. Chase undressing her—preparing her to take his cock deep inside her body. Standing half naked in her bra and panties, Larke sucked in a breath at the feel of his hands, cupping her breasts through her bra, lightly squeezing and weighing them. "Good thing I have large hands," he rasped beside her ear.

She swallowed hard, biting her lip as he unhooked the bra. Her breasts felt heavy and aching, with the tips pebble hard, straining towards him.

Her panties were the next to go. Chase kneeled in front of her, slid his strong hands up her thighs then with aching slowness peeled the undergarment down her legs. She stepped out of them. For the first time in her life, Larke stood completely naked in front of a man. Nude and aching with desire that only he could satisfy.

She looked at Chase, her eyes fixated on the sight of him rising to stand in front her. His gaze feasted on her. He made no qualms, blatantly perusing every inch of her naked body. Finally, he pinned his focus to hers and asked, his voice thick and husky. "Were those birth control pills I saw in your bathroom the other night?"

She nodded, feeling silly that he knew she was a virgin on the pill. "I've been taking them to help with period pains and my skin."

He gave a single nod, his heated gaze indicating he was more than satisfied with her answer. "The thing is, I can leave you here for a minute and go grab some condoms from my truck or you can trust me when I tell you I'm clean. I don't shoot up like some of the guys I know and you can believe me when I say I've never gone at it with a chick without using protection. I can swear on my own life. You're the only girl I wanna get real close to like that." His nostrils flared as his gaze shifted to her sex. "Wanna come really deep inside you, angel. I want you to be the first, only girl to take my seed."

Only me. Skin to skin. Larke whimpered, as his words sent shockwaves of titillating pleasure coursing through her. She wanted it all. Would take it all. His penis pumping inside her pussy, filling her to the brim with his semen. *God.* What that must feel like! Quivering with lust and anticipation she whispered, "I trust you."

Chase nodded and eased out of his clothes. Larke viewed him, rapt with fascination despite having already seen him in nothing but his boxers the night he'd spent at her place. She'd also seen naked men on television before but *this*… This was Chase. Hers. And she couldn't get enough of his ripped masculine frame. All corded muscles to her soft curves. Her gaze drifted downward. Larke stopped and almost swallowed her tongue at the sight of his shaft, breathtakingly thick and long. The glistening crown was red and wide…bobbing toward her.

Gorgeous. Was it even normal to consider a penis a thing of beauty? She didn't know, didn't care. Unconsciously she dabbed her tongue to her lips, wondering what the swollen head would taste like inside her mouth. Shaking herself, Larke inhaled deep. The ache between her legs was paramount, growing by the second. She tried to catch her breath, suddenly recalling the mild discomfort when Chase had first plunged his two fingers, thrusting inside her pussy. A tiny wave of panic seized her. She swallowed hard, looked up at his face then back down. There was only one thought inside her head. His massive, gorgeous cock was going to hurt her like nothing else.

Chapter Twelve

Chase watched as Larke lowered her eyes, gaping at his erection. She raised her gaze revealing dark eyes filled with raw desire. And fear. His dick was so hard, aching to relieve its tension inside her shapely body. Her skin was a flawless, smooth shade of dark brown. Her breasts were ripe and full, the nipples darker, almost black, compared to the rest of her body. The vision in front of him was everything that should've disgusted him, make his dick go limp.

Chase closed his hand over a breast, thumbing the beaded nipple. Larke was absolute perfection. That was the only way he could describe her. Inside and out, she was amazing, utter sweetness. When he noticed her eyes hesitantly shift to the tattoos on his upper body, his chest tightened, once again realizing how he must appear to someone as good as her.

Swallowing back his frustration, he cupped her face, kissing her lightly. " I want you to look at me—my face. Look at me and know how much you mean to me. Forget the tattoos. They don't mean a damn thing between the two of us." For the first time, Chase honest to God wished he wasn't covered in the hate-driven ink. That he wasn't about to penetrate his black girlfriend while she had to look at and run her hands over the racist symbols that showed his hatred for people like her.

She nodded and gave him a smile that made his heart hammer and his balls draw up. Chase wondered if maybe he'd been told so many awful things about race mixing to prevent him from feeling the way he did right now. Larke's smiling face, lashes lowered with desire and her rounded figure teasing him, telling him she was made just for him to spend hours upon hours holding on to her supple flesh while riding her, fucking her at his leisure. Coming over and over again, flooding her tight cunt with his cum. Overcome with the need to make her completely his, Chase lowered his head and captured a nipple between his lips. Her blunt fingertips grazed his scalp as she sighed softly.

His cock shot ramrod hard, cum churning inside his balls, desperate for release. Holding her by the hips, he hauled her up against him. She locked her legs around his waist as he cradled her to him and pressed forward for another kiss while caressing her curvaceous ass.

"I don't want to wait any longer," Larke said. She nuzzled the side of his face with her cheek. He laid her on the bed then grasped her at the ankles, parting her thighs wide. Chase groaned, racked with disbelief that she allowed him this tremendous pleasure. He eased between her legs, one hand on her hip, the other holding his cock with the heated tip pressed against her moist entrance. Stroking and caressing, he attempted to soothe her from the pain that was to come. Pressing forward, Chase pushed gently inside Larke's small opening.

She curled her fingers around his forearm. Her plump lips parted and a tiny whimper traveled across the room. Fuck. He wasn't even completely inside her and already she was in pain. Chase bit back a groan, because on his end, it felt so damn good. And that was just from her pussy squeezing the head of his dick. He took a deep breath, forcing the control he'd told her he had. The control he damn well better have when making love to the only girl who meant something to him.

"Does it hurt real bad?" He inhaled deeply, blocking out the voice screaming at him to pull out then thrust back in with a vengeance. Work the hottest pussy he'd ever been inside.

Larke shook her head and stroked his arm. "Good kind of pain." She rolled her hips. Her lids went low and her tone dropped lower, dripping with desire. "I can't believe we're doing this. It's starting to feel…" She sighed and bit her lip. "Wonderful. Like a dream."

A dream? Hell, he hadn't even started yet. Chase withdrew then thrust slowly, over and over until she clamped her legs hard around his hips. The sound of her low moans echoed inside the room. She bucked her hips, grounding against him like crazy. He grunted hard and held himself still, holding her waist, keeping her trapped beneath him. Unable to move. "Larke, baby. I know I told you I have a heap of control but I ain't no saint. If you keep grinding on me like that, I'm gonna end up fucking you hard. Might hurt a whole lot with you not used to having a dick inside your pussy at all."

Maybe Larke didn't fully understand what she doing, but either way, Chase growled his surprise as she raised her head and swept her tongue along his lips. "I can take you," she breathed. "I want to take you." She squirmed beneath his hold, working her body against his. Her erotic movements caused his cock to surge even deeper into her soaked pussy.

His control slipped. Within a split second, it was shredded. *Too good. Too much.* Chase withdrew, let out a harsh grunt then thrust hard, savage. Her cry of surprise was music to his ears.

"Uh," she cried over and over as he drove into her, balls deep and soaked in wetness. The bed dipped and wailed under the force of his thrusts. Beneath his own growls he could hear her crying out, "Oh God Oh God", in between shouts of his name. Larke's whimpering sent him over the edge. Her scream rose to a fevered pitch. Smooth thighs rubbed at his back. Her muscles clenched and unclenched, pulsating around his cock, buried deep within her channel. She was close to climax. He could bet his life on it. Larke was about to come because of *his* dick. The thought spurred him into frenzy. Chase couldn't help or stop himself from fucking her like a beast. It was all too much… That he could've been denied ever knowing the unimaginable pleasure between her thighs. Denied knowing her as the only woman for him. For him alone. His girl to treasure. He held her gaze, drinking in the sight of her head lolling back and forth, her braids fanned out on the bed. Larke's moans driving him insane as she came all around him.

Honeyed warmth flooded his cock, which was throbbing and swelling, pounding at her walls. He wouldn't last. Chase held her firm, pumping hard and fast. He groaned as shot after shot of cum jetted from his cock into her pussy. Soon after she had emptied him of everything, he hung his head to hers and kissed her lips.

The pounding in his heart eventually slowed to a normal pace. He looked down at Larke, realizing he hadn't stuck to his pledge. Her first time was supposed to have been gentle. Chase rolled to his side, noticing a speck of blood on his penis. Shit. Had he hurt her that badly? He glanced at her. She look…happy, even had her arms wrapped around his neck, smiling softly, like she was completely satisfied.

Easing away from her, he stroked her breast reassuringly because of the sudden flash of hurt on her face. "I'll be right back. Just going to the bathroom."

If he asked Larke she'd probably downplay her pain to spare his feelings. It was the kind of person she was. Chase strode into the bathroom, returning seconds later with a warm washcloth and knelt by the side of the bed.

"What are you doing?"

"Taking care of my lady." He crooked a finger, ignoring the surprise on her face. "Now come over here and open up. I know you got a bit of blood down there, Larke. You don't have to be shy."

She peered at him, hesitant. "It's fine. It's supposed to happen, right?"

"I guess. Ain't never had a virgin before. But I still wanna make sure I didn't hurt you too bad. I wasn't as gentle as I said I'd be. As I should've been." He gave her thigh a light swat. "Come on, angel, don't let me have to ask again."

Larke slowly parted her legs. It was wicked really. He was supposed to be doing this to care for her, but the sight of her damp folds gaping open for him, was so damn sexy. His cock twitched, hardening again in response to her pussy looking slightly puffy and a bit swollen, on account of his size and the rough way he'd gone at her.

Should feel bad.

He was an animal, simply because he *didn't* feel bad. In fact, Chase felt his chest swell with pride knowing she'd stretched to accommodate him. Only him. If he fucked her regularly, as he planned on doing, her tight little cunt would be molded to fit his cock like a glove. Aside from being swollen, he loved that her pussy was slick with traces of his semen glistening against her brown flesh. Red and brown. He swallowed hard, sobering at the tinges of blood.

Thankfully it wasn't a lot. He brought the cloth between her labia and pressed carefully, wiping away the fluids.

"Thanks," Larke whispered shyly.

Chase almost laughed at her shyness, considering she'd just given her virginity to him. Instead, he lowered his head and pressed a kiss to her center.

"Better?" He raised his head.

"Much," she said on a breathy moan.

After throwing the washcloth in the laundry basket, Chase noticed Larke had moved to the top of the bed and was underneath the covers. She was also lying on her side, with the other half of the sheets pulled down. Waiting for him. He shook his head and smiled as he climbed into the bed.

"What is it?"

"Nothing. I guess seeing you lying here gave me a weird feeling. Feels kinda cozy, sweet. A beautiful woman in my bed, waiting for me to join her for the night. Never had that before."

Her lips tilted upward into a smile. "So I'm the only girl you've spent the night with?"

"The entire night? Yeah. And I'm the only man you've had inside you *and* spent the night with. I'm happy. You?"

She chuckled low, her dark eyes sparkling. "Yes, Chase. I'm really happy. But now I feel dumb that I didn't pack something else."

"What?"

"Ear plugs for your snoring."

He gaped at her. He didn't snore. Did he? She laughed and poked him in the side. "You don't. I was playing. Plus if I needed something I'd simply use a pillow to keep you quiet."

Growling, he rolled over and grabbed her, tickling her sides. "Not funny. If you ever did something like that to me, you wouldn't be able to sit on that cute ass of yours for at least a week."

She giggled as he brought his hand to her ass, gently kneading. The laughter dissolved, giving way to lust flickering inside her eyes. She shifted closer, her fingertips holding on to his shoulder. "Chase?"

"Yeah?" He was running his hand below her belly button now.

"I'm getting wet again." She whispered it as if she was confessing a dirty secret.

He lowered his hand, slid a finger along her slit, finding her warm and slick. Ready for him again. Groaning inwardly, Chase forced himself to think with his head, the one on top of his body. "I know you want it. Me too. But I was rough before. You're gonna be hurting something real bad if I take you again so soon. Then I'll definitely break my word that I'd never hurt you."

Larke sighed then nodded. "I suppose you're right. It does hurt a little and I know it's important that you keep your word." She placed her arm around him again. He stroked and petted her clit. "Just cause I won't fuck you right now doesn't mean I can't still make you come."

Her eyes lit up as he got busy, fondling and fingering her pussy until she came all over his hand for the second time.

"What about you?" She brushed her fingers along his hard cock.

Chase took her hand, holding it to his chest. "I'm good. Don't worry about me. I can deal with a hard on. Tonight was all about you. Tomorrow, though… I'll start teaching you how to please me."

Chapter Thirteen

The next day, after lazing around in bed with Chase for the better part of the morning, Larke found herself in the middle of the woods. Instead of the thunderclouds she remembered from her last venture inside woodlands, there was nothing but golden rays of sunshine brightening the sky.

"So this is prime hunting ground?" she asked, listening carefully for wild animals.

"You could say that." Chase turned to her, one brow raised. "From the way you say it, I'm guessing you don't agree with hunting."

Didn't she? Larke shrugged. "When I hear the word hunting I have to be honest. It sounds a bit awful. Whether I agree or disagree. I can't really say because I don't know enough. I don't know anyone apart from you who does that."

"I was out hunting that day I saw you," he said, watching her closely. "I'd heard there was a wild hog roaming those woods. I sneaked out of the house while my folks were arguing, got my knife and thought I could find it and take it down by myself."

"Are you serious?"

He nodded with a wry grin. "Yep. Couple of weeks after what

happened to you and me, I heard one of the guys was out walking his dog close to that area. He got hurt seriously. That same boar attacked and punctured his lung. The worst is, he was twice my size, a grown man. Even the dog couldn't help him."

"Oh my God, Chase. That's horrible. Did he survive?"

"Yeah. He healed up just fine. But the thing is–if I hadn't seen you that day, I would've gone deeper into the woods. If I'd tried to take down that hog he probably would've ripped me to pieces. After everything that happened there, I didn't go anywhere near those woods for a while. The next time I went hunting, was a year later when I was twelve. I had to. Things were getting rough. We barely had any money. Gramps said the government stole most of it to hand out to minorities and was scaring new people from joining."

Larke thought about asking him if he really believed that but thought better of it. Deep down Chase had to know it wasn't a simple matter of favoring minorities. But what could she say? He chose to confide in her, trust her to hear him out and that meant so much right now. She wouldn't risk losing his confidence.

"Did you have to go hunting for food?" She prayed with all her heart that wasn't the case.

He chuckled low. The sound was harsh, devoid of any trace of humor. "I had to. It became every man for himself."

"But you weren't a man," she pointed out. "You were a child and I thought you'd lived with your mother and stepfather. They should've made sure you were taken care of." The more she learned about his family the more she despised them, even without the racism factor.

Chase shook his head. "I went back and forth staying with my grandfather and stepfather. Louise, my mother ran off while I was stuck in the sinkhole with you. Trevor had left to go looking for me–must have needed me to do something-and I guess she got fed up and decided to haul ass. Always said as much as she hated Jews and ni–black people, that she'd rather risk being around them than being holed up in Lee's Fortress catering to grown men."

Amid her heartbreak for the boy he'd been, Larke suddenly felt stupid. For some reason, she'd imagined it was only the males in Chase's life who were the hardcore white supremacists. But his mother? Lord. The woman must have been feeding him with hate since before he could talk. The thought made her blood boil and heart bleed.

"That shouldn't have happened," she cried, unable to hold her anger at bay. "You never should've had to go out and hunt for food if you had adults who were supposed to love and take care of you."

He gave her a sideways grin. "Maybe in your family, angel. Not mine. I stayed by myself for weeks at a time, so hunting was simply a new part of all that. Pretty much from that point on, I only hunted what I planned to eat. Don't see how it's any different than getting meat at the store or butcher."

Larke nodded, although her mind was no longer on the topic of hunting. Not after everything he'd revealed. She cleared her throat, trying not to dwell on the bleakness of his childhood before he picked up on her sadness and confused it for pity. Never pity.

"Do you ever take anyone hunting with you?"

He looked over at her as they went down a slope. "You mean if I've ever taken a female hunting. That's what you're asking, right?"

Her cheeks heated. *Found out.* "Since you put it out there like that, yes. I'm referring to other women."

"No. Can't say that I have. Never even thought about inviting anyone, to be honest."

"Hmm."

He grasped her hand where the slope got slippery, helping her to jump over a patch of mud. "What hmm? Are you trying to tell me you're interested?"

"I don't know. I'm not *not* interested."

He stared at her hard. "So you're interested?"

She squinted her eye at him. The man was so rational. "You're dragging things out of me, Chase Hudson. Making it hard for me to play coy. Since there's no beating around the bush with you, I'll be honest. Yes, I would like to tag along and hunt with you. I like meat."

He stopped in mid-stride, facing her with his features tense and brows raised. "You're not doing this to judge me?"

"No," she answered firmly. It was enough that one of them had issues with judging people. "I wouldn't do that." She gazed at him, deciding to test her limits. "It's not a good feeling believing someone is judging you, is it?"

Seconds ticked by with him staring at her long and hard. For a brief moment, she was afraid of his reaction. His features relaxed. "No," he said quietly. "It's not a nice feeling."

Larke smiled; relieved he'd thought the question through and answered honestly. When Chase turned to her with a boyish grin, her heart skipped a beat. "Apart from liking meat, why'd you wanna go hunting with me?" He pointed to her backpack, which was packed lighter than before. "If I take you with me next season, you can't bring that along. It's cute and all, but it ain't fit for hunting."

"I know." She really did. Talking to him yesterday had helped a lot. Planning and being prepared was okay, but sometimes a person needed to *not* be prepared. She hadn't expected Chase to enter her life, hadn't been ready or prepared for him, but here they were and it was the best thing that ever happened to her. Now they had each other.

His gaze washed over her and then he let out a deep sigh. "Larke. You know you're braver than I am, right? Hell, you took a chance with me, *after* finding out I'd been watching you on top of everything else. That night–when we were kids–I probably would've gone insane if I'd been in there with anyone else. You were so calm, even telling a story. You can handle anything that comes your way. If I'm not sure of anything in life, on this I know I'm dead right."

How to respond to that? Chase had such faith in her. Standing there with her heart inside her throat, Larke could only hope her actions showed him that she also believed in him. Somehow she managed to speak, whispering a throaty 'thank you' as they fell into silence, walking side by side.

There was no awkward moment. No struggle to make small talk. Only the peaceful feeling of knowing there was no need for noise, they were together, enjoying the other's company and that was enough.

After leaving the depth of the woodlands, they crossed into a path designated as walking trail. The mid-summer sun was high in the sky, breaking through the shade. The trail itself, along with the blue skies and simmering rays of sunlight hitting the ground, trees, and wildflowers peeking through the grass, reminded her of something out of a fairytale.

Larke contemplated stopping to take a couple of pictures on her phone. Perhaps it would provide inspiration for a new series idea she'd been toying with to present to her publisher. She shifted her head, ready to share her thoughts with Chase when a loud bark sounded from behind them. They both glanced backward, noticing a small chunky black and white pug coming up from behind them. The tag on its collar jingled.

Behind the dog was a little boy, running and crying out, "Jellybean, come back here! Stop." A short distance away they could both see a black woman who Larke assumed was the boy's mother, walking fast while pushing a stroller, calling out to the child and the dog.

As the pug attempted to whiz by, Chase reached out with smooth efficiency, grabbing a hold of its leash. Larke whistled, shaking her head with admiration. "You hunt, you carve knives and *stuff*, and now you catch runaway puppies."

He looked at her and grinned. "I'm good, right?"

She laughed and slapped his shoulder as the child came to up to them, his hand on his knee and panting. "Thanks, mister." He gazed up at Chase, who handed him the leash. "We got her a few days ago from the animal shelter. Didn't think she'd run away from me. And we just started training her too."

"It's cool. Better keep a tighter grip next time, kid."

The boy nodded, smiling at him. "Don't have to tell me twice."

"Jesus, Mikey. I told you to—"

The woman never finished whatever it was she had meant to say. She was in front of them now, her gaze flitting between Larke and Chase then centering on his tattoos. The boy's mother looked up. She was eyeing Chase with anger and disgust stretching across her face.

A fist tightened and gutted Larke deep in the pit of her stomach. The pain began to coil itself everywhere inside her body. Was this for the woman? Chase? Both. Larke wasn't sure. All she knew was, that woman who had the same skin color and was not much older than herself, had seen the symbols and read the words across Chase's arms for the first time. Larke remembered that pain. It was a deep one.

Beside her, she could feel Chase stiffen. She noticed the hardening of his jaw and the scowl on his face. Defensive mode. The woman inched backward, scooping one arm around her son, the other tightening around the handle of the stroller.

"Come on Mikey, let's go home."

Larke kept her eyes peeled to the woman hurrying off. She could hear the curt warning to the child, telling him he needed to keep a tighter hold on the leash. The woman then canted her head, peering over her shoulder, giving Larke a long puzzled stare. It was easy to understand the woman's confusion. If the tables were turned, Larke knew she would've done the same—wondering what the heck someone like her was doing with a man like Chase.

She sucked in a breath. The truth was, that woman and everyone else had no idea about the intricacy of her and Chase's relationship. Of course, it was unimaginable for them to understand that beneath the rough, white supremacist exterior, was a man who was growing and trying to change his ways. They wouldn't know that he was becoming her best friend and treated her with respect, caring and such tender affection that made her heart swell each and every day. And because of that, she needed to suck up the stares, toughen up and realize that things like this would happen more often than not.

While searching her mind for the right thing to say, Chase saved her the work by quietly asking, "Do you have any regrets, Larke?"

"A few," she answered truthfully. "I have a younger half-sister. My father remarried and his wife gave birth when I was around fourteen. They wanted me to fly out to Missouri to meet the baby and spend time with them. I refused. I had gotten used to him not being a physical part of my life and I suppose I was angry that he had a new family. At the time I didn't care how much my decision hurt him and his wife. My mom tried to convince me to go, but ultimately it was my decision. Looking back, I see how childish I'd been. We've all made up since then, and I love my little sister, but that was a selfish act I regret to this day."

He nodded. "You know the feeling. The thing is, I started getting these tattoos when I was a teen. Fifteen actually." He shook his head and let out a snort. "It's funny. Funny in a shitty kind of way, that of all the people I can talk to about this, it's you." He paused, his eyes appearing somber. "Or maybe not. Maybe it makes more sense than even I know, since as far as I can tell, you're the only person who understands or even care to *try* and understand me."

"You can always talk to me about anything," she said facing him. "Do you regret getting your tattoos?"

He was quiet for a while. He rubbed his forehead and said, "I'm not gonna stand here and lie to you that I'm a completely changed man or some crap like that. That wouldn't be fair. But I'm definitely trying to see things from a different angle. Understand more than I did before. As for the tattoos, yeah, I regret some of them. This right here on my arm. I can't get that image outta my head of you seeing it for the first time. Made me feel like absolute shit and I didn't know why I even cared what you thought. Last night I told you to forget about them, but it ain't that simple, is it?"

"No. It isn't," Larke agreed. "Did you also care when you saw how sad and scared that lady looked?"

"Cared? I don't know if that's the right word. I don't know her—don't wanna know her. But it didn't make me feel *good* to see that look on her face." He went quiet, appearing deep in thought. "Yeah. I guess in a way it did bother me."

"And it didn't before?"

"No. Never. Except for you." Chase drew in a breath. "If it wasn't so damn hot, I would've worn a long-sleeved shirt, like I did before when I figured out how much the tattoos bothered you."

Larke shook her head. "You can't go around covering them up all the time. Especially in summer. It's too hot like you said. For now, we'll just have to deal with it."

They continued along the path until he stopped in mid-stride, turning to her. "Did it upset you, what happened a while ago? Were you embarrassed?"

She bit her lip. "It upset me. The situation. Not you. I'm not angry with you. It's just upsetting that there are so many misunderstandings and misgivings out there. Like how you mentioned to me before that the government favors minorities. That's not true. Anything the government does for minorities is to try and put them on equal footing with white people. We're always a step behind because of our skin color. These programs only try to even the playing field. It's needed."

She raised her gaze to study his reaction. There was no usual hardening of his jaw or tick in his cheek. Larke continued. "There's a lot out there that's hard to understand for black and white people, everyone really. Take that little boy with the dog. I wonder if he saw those words on your arm—if he understood what they meant. And his mother, what happens when they get home? Will she have to explain it all to him? That'll be hard on her. Not only that but he'll also be confused, wondering why I was walking beside you. None of it will make sense to the child. So you see it's not a matter of embarrassment. Not at all. I'm not embarrassed to be with you or be seen with you. I care about you so much. I only wish this wasn't an issue between us. I don't want to feel like an exceptional black person. I'm no better than anyone else. I'm not gorgeous or brilliant. I'm just an average girl. A regular black person." She let out a deep breath and held out her hand, struggling for the right words to further explain her feelings. Words were too hard sometimes. "I don't know if what I said made much sense. All I know is I try to get along with everyone."

"I know," Chase murmured thickly. "Trust me, Larke, I know that's what you do. I have that necklace you gave me as proof. Been doing so ever since you were a little girl." He loped his arm around her waist. "I'm not trying to brush off anything you said but to me, there's nothing average about you. When I was in the bowling alley, before I heard your name, I couldn't take my eyes off you and that confused the hell out of me. When I realized you were the same girl I'd met as a kid, it was like something went off inside my head and I knew why I was reacting the way I was. You were the first person to be kind to me and I guess that kind of stuck with me on some level. About everything else you said—I get it. I really do, angel and I'm working on myself. I can't make promises, but I'm not gonna be like a fucking moron and make decisions based on everything I was taught to believe."

She clasped her hand to his, the love she was beginning to feel for him blossomed inside her heart. "That's all I can ask for right now."

Chapter Fourteen

Chase was talking too much. He'd gone all his life priding himself on being smart enough not to trust anyone. Not to depend on anyone. But Larke was messing it all up, turning the world he knew upside down and everything he was familiar with into chaos. Simply by being her wonderful, caring self. Talking about his childhood wasn't something he normally did. He didn't have friends, and if he did, he sure as hell wouldn't have felt comfortable telling anyone about being so poor he'd had to go hunting for his own damn food.

The look on Larke's face as he'd told her, however, made him realize she'd never considered before that a kid would have to resort to such extreme measures. Her innocence to his harsh reality was another reason for him to rethink the things he'd learned. Somehow, it no longer seemed true that being white made him or anyone else more civilized than all the other races. While Larke was living her nice life with a mother who cared about her, he was the skinny white kid out by himself hunting in the woods with a growling stomach and wearing dirty clothes.

It was all just plain wrong. So much that he didn't want to think about it for now. In fact, Chase shoved it all together from his mind. He was with his girl and the last thing he wanted was another issue to come up between them, like earlier today because of that damn dog.

Glancing over at Larke, he noticed that she was struggling to eat the Chinese Takeout they'd ordered on the way home. She was determined to use chopsticks although it seemed her hand and the utensil refused to get along. She picked up a piece of meat and slowly tried bringing it to her opened mouth. Her brows furrowed in concentration. The beef got as far as the edge of her bottom lip before the chopsticks fell.

Chase wanted to laugh and hug Larke for being her regular self, but at the same time, he felt the urge to grab the chopsticks and order her to eat the food with the fork because they weren't in goddamn Asia. He kept quiet. Chase got up and went to her. Crouched by her knee, he took the chopsticks and placed them between her fingers. "It's like this, angel." He kept his hand over hers, guiding her motion to keep the chopsticks and the food from falling.

"I feel dumb," she said jokingly before using them on her own without any food falling.

Chase returned to his spot on the couch and chuckled. "Don't. I only figured it out cause I ordered some noodles once and they sent chopsticks with it. I had time to kill while I was waiting to meet up with…" He caught himself and shut his mouth. Larke was making him talk too much again. Saying things she had no business knowing and would only upset and hurt her.

Not surprisingly, she laid the chopsticks on the coffee table, her eyes suddenly sad. "I was watching a documentary the other day. It was about hate groups." His entire body grew tense. She noticed it, yet kept on talking. "I know it's not something we've ever sat down and discussed, but we have to. The program was about the largest hate group in America. Of course I started thinking about you, how you mentioned going to different places. Then I got scared and worried. Angry too. That I definitely have to admit. I was upset, thinking of you going to those racist events I saw in the documentary. There were so many horrible things said and joked about. I didn't want to think about you doing that sort of thing with your group. All I want is the truth, Chase. When you mention driving across states, does that involve going to gatherings? Do you ever make plans to harm anyone?"

The feeling of a knife slashing into him hit Chase hard. He swallowed, finding it hard to speak. "Do you think I've hurt anyone?"

Larke gave him a sad look that made him want to pound his fist against a wall in self- disgust. "No," she finally whispered. "My heart told me you hadn't, but I needed to hear it straight from you."

"I keep to myself, Larke. You know that. But that doesn't mean I'll hesitate to protect myself."

"And the gatherings?"

He couldn't lie to her. "We don't do anything as big as some of the other groups but all of the members get together at least once a year. We also have other local events scattered throughout the year. As for why I go away sometimes, it's not because of any big gathering or committing crimes."

"Then why? Please tell me."

He shoved a hand through his hair and bounded out of the chair. She was watching him. Her eyes were huge, boring into his and pleading with him to confide in her. He should shout at her, Chase reasoned. Remind Larke that this part of his life was none of her damn business. None of the girls he'd ever messed around with would dare to ask him so many questions.

Letting out a growl of pent up frustration and knowing that in the end, he was powerless against her pleas, Chase bit out, "I meet up with people who you wouldn't even *begin* to suspect had ties to groups like mine. I'm not gonna give any names. Don't ask me to. But some of these guys, I can tell you, you definitely won't sleep better at night knowing what they think about the people they're supposed to help, serve, represent and educate. They're our big donors. Not just AR, they give money to white supremacist groups all over the country. These are people who don't mind handing out cash if they think it's gonna help lead America in a certain direction. Our job is to keep that confidence alive by doubling, tripling our membership all the fucking time. Now, I hope you're happy because that's all I'm gonna say on this. No more questions, Larke. I mean it." He drew in a breath, calming his nerves and lowering his voice at the frightened expression on her face. "Angel, this is *not* the type of thing I wanna discuss with you."

She nodded and continued to stare at him, her eyes misty as if she was trying to keep from crying. "Do you think I asked because I'm nosey?"

Of course he didn't. But he also didn't know why she cared about where he went. "I don't think that, but I'm confused why you even care if I leave for a couple of days at a time. I'm gonna come right back to you every single time."

She gazed up at him, eyes still watery. "I only asked because I'd be so worried about you, wondering what you were doing. If you were safe or doing things you would regret." She closed her eyes. "I thought it would be obvious."

His heart pounded as he bent to press his lips to her cheek. "Not to me, it isn't." Things like that would never be obvious to a guy like him. The same guy who had worried for years about his mother, only to track her down and have her reject him like a sorry dog, by warning him to stay the fuck away from her because she had a new life. One that didn't include taking care of a seventeen-year-old.

Larke rose from the couch and stroked her palm against his face. "Chase, I care about you. In my world when someone means a lot to you, that also includes worrying about them and wanting them to be safe. And I worry a whole lot." She reached for his hand. "With caring also comes trust. I'll trust you and you'll trust me because I won't ever betray you. In any way shape or form."

She's breaking me.

Chase's throat felt lumpy. "I've gone a long time without needing anyone to trust, what makes you think I need this from you?" He closed his hand over her own, unsure if he was smiling or scowling. Larke had him so messed up inside, feeling all kinds of nervous. "Wasn't like I planned on telling you everything about me. That just won't happen. I might let something slip here and there but those aren't real secrets." *Not like the horrible, shameful, ones I have. Too scared to tell you even though I trust you with my life.*

Her lips widened as her finger scorched a path down his chest. "You'll need this from me because sooner or later you'll feel like bursting. Holding it all in isn't good for anyone. I used to be a nurse, so you should definitely listen to me. And…if you don't have any real secrets, Mr. Hudson, you do have a heart, mind and *real* emotions. Those things feed on, absolutely thrive on connections. An intimate, compassionate, thoughtful connection. That's what I have to offer. It's also what I expect from you. When the time comes and you're ready to lay your soul bare, I'll be here to help you sort it all out."

"You don't know what you're talking about," he whispered, fighting down the gravel inside his throat. Larke was doing a number on him. Reading him so damn well. Offering everything he wanted. Despite his denial, Chase found himself holding on to her. He let go of her hand to caress her thigh.

"I'm right, aren't I?" she insisted, her voice taking on a husky edge. "You don't want to admit it. But you will. In time."

"In time," he repeated, barely able to think now. His cock became

painfully hard. "While you're waiting on that prediction to happen, I'm here waiting on something else."

Her eyes softened. "You are?"

"Yes. My dessert."

He could see the pulse in her neck throb. "We have ice cream in the freezer."

If Chase wasn't hurting so bad he'd actually smile at her attempt to play innocent.

"Not talking about anything cold."

"No? Perhaps you should show me what you have in mind and um, I'll do my best to make it warm."

Game over. Maybe if he was a different man, he could've continued playing along with her silly game. He wasn't. Chase moved in front of her, blocking her space to make sure she understood he was no longer in the mood for joking. "Take off your clothes and sit on the table."

"The table?" she echoed, her eyes widening.

"Yeah. That table." His tone was harsher than intended as he pointed to the dining room table.

Without another word, Chase stood back and observed her undressing before sitting on the table as he'd instructed. He knelt in front her, grasping her legs until they rested on his shoulders.

"This is what I've been waiting for all day." Larke's gasp thundered across the room the moment he spread her folds and slid his tongue along her slit. Warm and wet and so fucking sweet. A thousand times better than all that candy they'd eaten together.

With every lash of his tongue, she bucked her hips off the table. Chase held her firm, sucking her clit and dipping his tongue into her pussy.

"Ohh." She gripped the edge of the table, holding firm. Above him, Chase could hear the faint sound of her teeth gnashing together. The grating turned into soft little moans, followed by Larke sobbing his name over and over, begging him not to stop.

Driving him insane.

If his cock wasn't rock hard and demanding attention, he'd be happy spending the entire night between her legs, lapping at her hot little pussy. *His* hot little pussy.

When her body began to tremble and her cries began coming out in ragged pants, Chase made a mental note to remind Larke at some point that she was his, belonged to him. Delicious wetness warmed and slid over his tongue. He didn't stop. He held her throughout her climax, licking slowly while gently kneading her hips.

"Better?" He dropped a kiss to her center then raised his head, gazing at her.

She let out a sound somewhere in between a moan and a laugh then buried her face in the crook of his neck. "A thousand times better. Just like last night."

Larke lifted her face. Her eyes flickered with lust as she looked down to the tented front of his jeans. She ran her toes over his erection. "Are we each supposed to get a dessert?"

Chase stood between her legs now, eyeing her carefully. "Depends on what exactly it is you're craving?"

Her eyes suddenly went hazy with lust. So much it almost made him weak. "You. Something hard. Hot. I want to know what you taste like." She swept her tongue across her bottom lip. "Can I lick you, like you did me? Take your penis inside my mouth?"

God in fucking Heaven. Was this really happening? Chase drew in a breath. His cock throbbed and twitched. He rubbed the head through his pants, squeezing it out of fear he'd come before she even touched him. And that was insane. He'd gotten his dick sucked lots of time before, but this…Damn. This was different. Larke was actually *asking* for permission to put her precious, innocent lips on him. Him!

He cleared the lump from his throat but it was still hard to speak. So he didn't try. Chase helped her from the table and clasped her to his chest, just because it felt so damn good. When he gained control, enough for him to speak clearly, he thumbed the corner of her lips and asked, "You've never done this before, have you?"

She shook her head, viewing him through lowered lashes. "No. This isn't something I'd do or *want* to do with just anyone." She bit her lip again, appearing shyer than ever. "I've read about it in books and magazines of course."

He smiled at her then found himself saying something, that months ago he would've never uttered to a female willing and waiting to please him with her mouth.

"It'll be different than in a magazine or book, Larke. I'm sure you know that. Just…" Chase paused. Scrubbed his hand along his jaw. "Listen, I don't want you to think you *have* to do this. Like I was expecting it or something. But if at any point you don't wanna keep your mouth on me, then stop, okay. I won't be angry. I'll probably still be hard as hell," he said half-jokingly, "but I won't be mad. I don't want you doing anything that you don't like or doesn't feel right."

"That's very sweet, Chase. And I'll keep that in mind. But right now, I want to please you as you pleased me." Larke swept her lips across his stomach then fell to her knees in front of him, flicking her long braids over her shoulder. His dick jerked at the innocent yet erotic gesture.

Her fingers easily went to work opening his pants. When her hands brushed over his cock, holding the base inside her fist, Chase kept his eyes riveted to her, wanting to savor every second of seeing his girl with her cheeks full, pleasing him with her mouth.

She darted her gaze upward, stuck out her pink tongue and laved it along the length. Again and again, she licked, real slow then fast. Chase groaned and tilted his head back. Her mouth, so close to his cock caused pre-cum to spill from the tip.

She licked it off, dipping her tongue into the slit. "You taste good," she whispered, raising her eyes to his face. "Really. Really good."

Oh Fuck. His cock pulsed within her hand. Chase raked his fingers through her braids, wrapping a handful around his fist. "Ahh, Larke. I can't take anymore. Suck it from the top, angel. Show me how much you like the taste of my dick."

Her eyes fluttered close. She rocked on her heel, letting out a low moan before closing her mouth around the entire head. Chase grunted low in his throat. Her mouth felt hot and moist, pulling him in, sucking, sucking.

Larke lifted her head and stared at him. His words came back to haunt him. Damn, maybe she didn't like his cock after all. Drawing in a breath he forced his nerves to calm. Before he could ask, she shook her head, licked the crown then grated, "I love it. Just needed some air." She lowered her mouth and closed her lips over him, sucking slow and good. Head tilted back with eyes half closed, Chase pumped slowly into her mouth. "Can you try to take me deep?" He was desperate to feel his cock hitting her throat.

She gave a small nod. He could hear the shallow intakes of breath through her nostrils. The tips of her fingers stroked his balls, massaging them as she sucked him deep, near but not all the way to the back of her throat. She held him there, rocking back and forth, her eyes glued to his. She parted her lips, allowing him to slip from her mouth as she gulped another breath of air.

Chase tightened his fist around her braids, holding her to him as his heart slammed against his chest. All the while she rubbed her lips against his cock, trying to catch her breath. "You want more?" he whispered, dying of pleasure each time her lips brushed against the pre-cum slickened tip.

She nodded and flattened her tongue over the tip. "Want to make you come."

He groaned as she started sucking again. "Almost there, angel. Almost there. Keep that up and I'm gonna come real hard." He glanced down at her, his breathing harsh, strained. "I'll... give you a warning."

She nodded, cupped his balls, squeezing and weighing them in her palm while her mouth worked his cock over and over until Chase could hold nothing back. Blood pumped through his blood and roared in his ears. Since it was her first time, he pushed her head back, pulled his dick from her mouth, watching as cum laced from the swollen head, spilling across her breasts, wetting her nipples.

He kept coming, looking at the sight and almost sinking to the floor when she stared at his seed, her dark eyes brimming with fascination. Their gazes met and held. Larke dipped a fingertip to her breast then brought it to her mouth, sucking off the trace of semen.

Dying. Dying. She's tasting my cum.

"No warning next time," she said breathlessly. Lowering her head, she drew him back into her mouth, sucking and licking his dick clean. Afterward, reeling and shaking from the force of his orgasm and Larke's tenderness, Chase dropped to his knees on the floor, threw his arms around her naked body and held tight with one thought in mind. *She's mine.*

Chapter Fifteen

On the last morning of their time together in Lake Walnut, they awoke at the crack of dawn and spent the morning lazing around between the sheets, making love then showering together. Larke smiled as she recalled the showering part, being pressed up against the tiles of the shower wall with Chase moving so deep inside her. Showering alone would forever pale in comparison, she decided.

During the drive home, it was hard not to feel sadness at the return to reality. Being around Chase was addicting and it had been all too easy getting used to the feel of him next to her in bed at nights. After he'd dropped her off and helped bring her bags into her apartment, Larke was glad to have found some measure of comfort in his promise that nothing between them had changed because they were back home. They'd see each other again and often too.

"If you ever call me and I don't pick up right away, it's not cause I'm ignoring you. Just bad timing."

Chase had said that an hour ago, right after he'd hauled her against him, kissing the breath right out of her body. She touched her lips, still tasting his kiss. Sighing, Larke looked over at the clock. The reading she'd had scheduled at a local library was in a half an hour. She gave herself a quick once over then grabbed her sweater in case the air conditioning was being blasted inside the building.

"Oh good, you're here."

She'd barely stepped through the door of the library before Mrs. Downing, the middle-aged blonde librarian she'd been corresponding with for the past two weeks, pulled her inside.

"Am I late?" Larke checked her watch.

Mrs. Downing shook her head. "No, you're not. But look over there. I didn't realize so many children would show up. They're getting antsy waiting for you to start reading."

Larke followed the older woman's gaze to see that the area they'd designated for the reading was pushed even further back to accommodate all the children who had shown up. She gasped in disbelief. "Here I was hoping not to be embarrassed with only one child showing up."

Mrs. Downing brought her hands together. "Larke. Please, please, please tell me you don't mind starting early?"

"No not at all," she assured Mrs. Downing, while taking another glance at the children chattering excitedly. "I still can't believe this."

"Well believe it. Your books are popular here. As they should be. You have a fantastic imagination. Now, before it gets rowdier in here. Can you start the reading?"

Larke took her seat in the front of the room. Since becoming a published writer, this was her first time doing a public reading. Her stomach felt nervous and fluttery. It wasn't only children staring at her, also adults who were probably secretly rolling their eyes. She wasn't sure if she should be annoyed or thankful for the ones who had their gazes cemented to the screens of their smartphones.

Drawing in a deep breath, she introduced herself and shortly began reading. Halfway through the book, as she paused for dramatic effect–when the badger suddenly found himself in a sticky situation after abandoning his friends–Larke raised her head to notice a well-dressed man staring at her with a smile on his face. Lowering her head, she continued reading. After saying that glorious phrase "The End", she sank back in her chair. Relief flooded her as the children clapped and started talking to each other about the characters in the book. Shortly after, when the children slowly began piling out and around the library, she felt even lighter.

Whew. She'd done it! And without her voice cracking from nerves. Larke reached for her bag, reminding herself that next time she'd try not to feel so nervous. Although the butterflies inside her stomach finally settled, Larke found herself jumping, startled by a voice behind her.

"I'm sorry. I didn't mean to scare you."

"It's fine," she said. It was the man who had been staring at her during the reading.

"My daughter enjoyed the reading very much. She loves your books, especially this one with the badger's new friend. We read them often."

"I'm glad to hear that. Thank you, both for coming out." She issued him a polite smile then shifted her attention to her bag, expecting him to leave. He didn't. "This might be forward of me, but you are a very beautiful lady."

Larke blushed. She felt awkward. The man was handsome, he honestly was. Smooth, patient voice and brown skin with an infectious smile. On outward appearance, he was exactly the type of person she would've wanted to date. But…Chase. He was the only man for her. He had her feeling like she was soaring high above the clouds whenever she thought of him. Larke prayed the man beside her wasn't working up this intro to ask her out.

"You wouldn't be available to go out with me sometime, would you? I mean, if you can find time away from your busy schedule."

Oh no. Her palms suddenly moistened with sweat. She'd never had to turn anyone down before. No one decent that was. Larke closed her bag, shaking her head inwardly. For some reason, her heart felt heavy despite this man being a stranger. Like turning him down was wrong on so many levels.

"I can't," she murmured, slightly ashamed of herself. "I'm in a relationship."

He snapped his finger and gave her an exaggerated look of disappointment. "Always too late with the pretty ones."

She forced a smile to her lips, unsure what to say when dealing with an irrational sense of guilt and shame. She held out her hand then allowed it to fall by her side.

Her shoulders finally relaxed after the man gave a single nod and left without pursuing his interest further. Despite all that, Larke found herself staring at his back. No, she wasn't attracted to him. Maybe she would have been—at some other point in time, before her connection with Chase. She didn't know. But attraction wasn't the root of her unease. Biting her lip, Larke leaned her head against the wall, staring straight ahead, unseeing.

Race Traitor.

That was the only word to describe her. Exactly what she was, Larke silently chastised herself. Oh, she didn't subscribe to the belief that people had to stick to their own race. For someone like her, however, to choose… No, to be on the verge of falling in love with a man whose body was covered with the symbols of his prejudiced beliefs and hate. *That* was a betrayal. Surely that made her a dirty race traitor. Didn't it?

Larke gulped as a wave of self-disgust so strong made her stomach roil and filled her with nausea. But worse than that, not even the horrid wave of guilt was strong enough to quell her desire for Chase or curtail the feelings inside her heart. Either she was a very twisted person or stronger than she'd ever imagined for heeding the natural instincts that told her they belonged together.

Instead of heading straight home that day, Larke found herself knocking on Riva's door. While she was away at Lake Walnut, her friend had called her multiple times. Larke knew she was concerned.

Going away with a guy was beyond anything she'd ever done before and her friend knew it. And frankly, Larke was tired of keeping her relationship with Chase a secret. She was bubbling inside, on the verge of bursting from wanting to tell someone about the path life seemed intent on steering her.

Riva opened the door, excitedly pulling her inside. "Good. You're back from your rendezvous."

Larke grinned as she entered her friend's living room. While other kids had teased her in middle school because of her weight, Riva was one of the few girls who'd never had a mean thing to say about Larke, instead choosing to be a close friend to this day. The Indian girl was always truthful, adding a bit of humor to get her point across.

"I got back this morning."

Riva sat on the couch with her legs folded, staring at Larke with anticipation. "Do I need to get popcorn ready? It's not every day I get all the details about you *finally* having a man." The raven-haired young woman shook her head. "I'm for real. I don't know how you do it, going forever without having had sex." She narrowed her gaze on Larke. "Wait a minute. If you were away with this mystery guy, please, for Heaven's sake tell me you got laid. As your friend, I'm very much concerned you'll one day end up with cobwebs inside your vagina."

"That's disgusting," Larke muttered. She'd been hearing that from Riva for over two years now.

"Well it's true, and I'm still a practicing nurse, unlike you. I should know." Riva leaned closer to her. "Anyways. What's up? By what's up I mean tell me everything about your new man. My life is boring. I need excitement from other people."

Larke gazed at her friend, wondering if she'd made a mistake believing she could confide in her about such a touchy subject. Feeling silly and afraid she'd be lectured about falling for a guy so quickly, she shook her head. "It's nothing interesting."

Riva stared at her, disbelief written on her face. She said nothing at first, then finally pointed out, "We've been friends since we were twelve. I think I know you well enough to recognize when you're saying one thing, but your eyes and face say another."

"You noticed all of that?"

"I sure do. Now tell me what's wrong. Did something happen while you were away with him?"

"His name is Chase," Larke answered quietly. "He's also not a mystery man. You've seen him before." She blew out an unsteady breath. "Remember that guy we saw in the bowling alley, the one at the counter when everyone got real quiet."

Riva opened her mouth in shock. "Your mystery man is Davey, the clerk?"

Maybe at some other time she would've found that funny. "No, not him."

Riva frowned. "The only other guy was that…" Her near jet black eyes widened into orbs. "Are you serious?"

"Don't look like that," Larke begged her friend. Her throat felt clogged fearing Riva would tell her she was a horrible person. Riva didn't. She scooted over and placed her arm around Larke's shoulder. "What happened? I won't make any jokes. Talk to me."

Larke did. She poured her heart out, excluding the intimate and personal details she knew Chase would not appreciate her sharing.

"Seeing that black guy in the library made you feel like a bad person?"

Larke nodded. "Do you think I am?"

"We both know you're not a bad person. I'm not a psychologist, but I think anyone in your position would feel some form of guilt. You shouldn't beat yourself up about it, especially since you and Chase have a history."

"I wasn't planning to," Larke told her. "I couldn't because whatever guilt I feel doesn't compare at all to how hard I'm falling for Chase."

Riva pursed her lips. "Do you think he's in love with you?"

"I don't know." *I hope so.*

"I mean if the two of you were in love then none of this white supremacy stuff would be an issue anymore, right? He'd leave it all behind for you." Riva eyed her carefully before adding. "Larke, he'd have to."

All evening long after she had left her friend's apartment, Larke thought back to what Riva said. *He'd have to.*

It was the obvious truth. Chase had to know this too. She hoped he did.

Chapter Sixteen

The first thing Chase noticed when he walked inside Trevor's house was the pungent scent of cigarettes, vomit, and alcohol. He stepped over a couple empty cans of beer and made his way out to the back, where he could see wafts of smoke curling into the air. Chase glimpsed the kitchen table on his way out. Thankfully there was no sign of meth since it seemed Trevor was determined to spend his last days, weeks, months, whatever amount of time he had left in a haze of self-indulgence.

Chase wished he could spend more time doing as he pleased because all he wanted was to be with his girl right now instead of *here*. Sure he'd seen Larke regularly since coming back from Lake Walnut two weeks ago, but damn, even regularly wasn't enough. Because that meant sometimes he'd go a day or two between seeing her.

He pushed the sliding doors apart and was soon outside, standing next to Trevor. His stepfather's face was thinner than the last time Chase had seen him, which was three days ago. The skin appeared to droop over whatever flesh was left underneath.

Trevor took a draft of the cigarette and turned to him, a grin on his now ugly face. "Ain't nothing like going out doing what a man loves best, huh?"

Chase forced a chuckle. "No females?" Sadly there were some in Antebellum Resistance who would still fuck Trevor, even in this condition.

"Like-minded, ain't we son?" He threw the cigarette butt on the ground, beside an already growing pile. "You'll soon learn that as capitán here, there's always an unlimited supply of bitches willing to—"

Chase cut him off. "There's only one female I got my eyes on," he muttered, speaking the truth out of annoyance. "You got any news from the doctors how things are going?" he asked, changing the topic.

Trevor snorted. "Nope. Just waiting around to meet my Maker. And ready to hear you say you can handle the job hundred percent. Got the feeling you're iffy about it all. Maybe I'm wrong. Hope I'm wrong," he added with emphasis. "I'd sure hate to go through them pearly gates o' Saint Peter's and have to explain to Joe why his beloved grandson is too pussy to take over the greatest movement this side of the Mississippi."

Chase stared at Trevor. The truth was, some days he wasn't sure he believed in Heaven despite religion having been crammed down his throat as a boy. Instead of learning math and science he'd been learning how God created different races for a reason and that inter-mixing them was direct opposition and slap in the face of God's will.

But the innocent reporter his grandfather killed... That had to be the most blatant disregard for God's will. He knew the Ten Commandments. Knew right from wrong. What was legal from illegal. Why had they chosen to obsess about race of all things? Why would murder be acceptable but treating other races with respect, not?

Chase couldn't stop himself from asking, "Don't you ever wonder if you, me, any of us, really, would actually get past those gates on the other side. I mean, we're not complete saints, right?" His own silence about a horrible crime surely meant he was going to hell. Where his grandfather was and more than likely where Trevor was headed...if such a place existed.

Trevor let out a harsh laugh. "Since when you become a goddamn preacher?" He laughed again. "Fuck no, I ain't never wondered no bullshit like that. Heaven was created for us, Chase. God knows we're suffering some kinda hell down here and ZOG is the devil, tormenting white people. That's why…"

Chase wasn't sure when it happened but at some point, all the slurs, talks of a Zionist occupied government became like white noise. His mind was blocking it all out. Trevor's voice remained in the background, like the low hum of a machine running. Chase was so tired of hearing the conspiracy theories and arguments about why non-whites were useless and a danger to society. Whether there was truth to any of it, somehow no longer seemed important or valid enough to center his entire life around.

When Trevor's mouth finally stopped moving, he thought about reminding the man that at the end of the day, it was his own bad habits that led to his downfall—upcoming death. He, Trevor and no one else. But because of who he was, how he was raised, Chase kept quiet. No amount of talking would lure Trevor from his 'truths'.

Also, like it or not. Chase knew he had a role to fulfill. One that had been chosen for him and no amount of pretending would change it.

The blood of his ancestors ran deep inside of him. He was a born and bred racist, an animal with a legacy to carry on. It wasn't a matter of saying "Fuck it, I'm out" and walking away. Too many eyes were on him, expectations, hope, and goddamn trust that he would lead them. They were all waiting on him to stand between them and the threats from the Jewish controlled government and all the brown people who were beneath them.

It hurt even thinking that. Larke was so far from being beneath him. If anything, she was *above* him. He knew it and was positive she did too. She was his better half. Plain and simple. An asshole like Trevor would never understand that because he wouldn't want to.

"If the doorbell rings, it'll probably be one of them females you mentioned, coming over."

Chase blinked, drawing himself out of his thoughts. He realized what Trevor was saying. "Serious?"

Trevor grinned. His yellowed teeth gleamed. "Not for me. Wish I could. Mind's willing but the body just ain't having it. It's for you. Bet you thought I was joking when I said you needed a proper woman."

"Who is she?"

"Haley. Heard she has a thing for you. She's cute enough. Has some Italian blood in her but that ain't an issue. I talked with her the other day. She wants you real bad, man." He flicked a hand in the air. " Go get that ass."

Torn between disgust and amusement, Chase heard the doorbell ring exactly as Trevor had predicted.

Snorting, he looked behind at Trevor who had his eyes closed and another cigarette between his lips. Chase strode through the house to the front door. He opened it and sure enough, Haley was standing there. His gaze dropped from her face to her body. She was dressed nicely, wearing a red midriff that allowed him a view of her flat stomach and tiny waist along with white shorts, stopping just below her ass. If she'd dressed to entice him it wasn't working. His dick was dead when it came to any female apart from his girl. Knew who it belonged to.

Haley's red lips spread into a smile. "How's it going?"

"It's going. Same as always."

She nodded slowly, her gaze coursing over him. "Can I come in? Trevor invited me over. He said maybe you and I should get to talking. He thinks we might have…things in common."

"Trevor's mistaken."

She frowned. "Why do you say that? I don't think I've made it a secret that I'm interested in you. I even saw that you called me back last month. I tried calling you a couple of times again, but I guess you were busy and we never found the right time."

I've been ignoring you. For a second Chase thought about just telling her the plain truth. Him calling her that time had been a mistake. He'd been confused because of seeing Larke and finding himself attracted to her. All he'd wanted was to use the opportunity of easy sex that Haley would've offered, to try and erase Larke from his mind. It wouldn't have worked and Chase was glad he'd hung up the phone before Haley had answered.

But the thing was, Haley wasn't necessarily a bad person. She, like the rest girls who grew up here, was like him. They'd all grown up hearing the same stories, told what their duties were, where their loyalty rested. She barely knew him to have any real feelings for him, apart from wanting a nice hard fuck.

And now, with Trevor about to die, she knew he was next in line to lead one of the biggest neo-Confederate groups in North Carolina and wanted to be his girl. Yeah. No. Just no to fucking all of it.

Chase pinned her with a hard stare. "Listen. I know you think what you're doing is good. Thing is, there's not gonna be anything between us. I don't care what Trevor told you. As a matter of fact, he's right around back. You probably hear the coughing, so I'm sure he'll need your attention more than I do."

"I didn't come here to see Trevor," Haley argued. She titled her head to the side and raised her hand to touch him. The look on his face must have been warning enough because she immediately lowered it. "Well what do I say to Trevor?" she asked fearfully.

Chase raised his brows. This was insane. "Tell him I was an ass to you. As a matter of fact, you don't need to tell him shit. Trevor can't do anything and he doesn't control you or any of us."

She shifted her leg. "I-I guess you're right. He *is* dying."

Afterward, Chase shook his head as he climbed into his truck and watched Haley leave. It wasn't normal that any of them should feel so controlled. Himself included. He then drove the short distance to his house. Inside the room he had set up as a work area of sorts, Chase tried and failed to concentrate on what exactly he wanted to do with the pieces of wood laid out in front of him. He set the chisel aside and glanced at all the items he'd carved in the past months. He'd never shown any of it to anyone. Not since he was a kid and his grandfather had found him with his chisel attempting to carve a deer. The old man had taken the piece and smashed it against the wall. *You ain't no goddamn fairy. Don't let me see you sitting here making pretty toys. You like deer, go out and fucking kill one.*

Chase pushed the memory aside. He still didn't get what carving had to do with being soft or homosexual. That's why he'd continued doing it as a kid, in secrecy, hiding the items he'd crafted in the back of his closet as he'd done with the necklace Larke had given him.

Now it's Larke I'm hiding. Shame and nausea roiled in his gut. When his phone rang, Chase reached for it. It was Larke. For a second he contemplated not answering, afraid she would somehow be able to read his thoughts, hear the shame and guilt when he spoke. But of course. He answered, because fuck. It was Larke and he wanted to hear her voice so much and see her even more.

She was on her way home from running errands, so Chase suggested they meet somewhere in between. Both agreed on the plaza a couple of miles away. Right away after reaching the square, he spotted her dark green sedan in the parking lot and pulled up in the spot next to hers, which was in front of a hunting store. She'd texted him minutes before that she wanted to check out the place while waiting for him.

Chase smiled to himself as he pushed through the door. It made him feel good knowing how serious she'd been about wanting to hunt with him next season. The place was almost empty with no cashier in sight. He wasn't surprised. Although this wasn't the hunting store he'd worked at some years ago, he'd visited this one before and knew it was filled with lazy ass workers who were never around when anyone needed them. He strode toward the back of the store, lightly skimming the walls for anything interesting while keeping an eye out for Larke.

He didn't see her right away but he did hear a voice—McNair's. Immediately, Chase remembered McNair was also a big hunter. Still, there was no way he could've expected the other man to be here today. Now.

"What do you need help finding?" McNair asked. He was leaning against the wall mere inches from Larke, a smug grin on his face.

"I don't need help," she said. "All I want is for you to give me some space."

Chase moved closer, anger simmering in his blood at the look on McNair's face. It was the same taunting look *he'd* had on his face that night in the parking lot, when he'd toyed with Larke despite knowing she was afraid.

Chase saw the exact moment Larke glanced across the aisle and became aware of his presence. Her gaze caught his, yet she made no attempt to speak or go to him. She glanced at McNair again, mainly at his bare shoulder, which bore the same Confederate flag standing tall amid the fire and ashes tattoo. She was now looking between the two of them. A bite to the lip. Chase could swear he saw the pulse in her neck racing.

McNair broke the silence, turning to face him. "Hey Hudson. Lookie what I got here. Haven't seen one of them in here in a long time. You?"

Chase ground his teeth, forcing himself to remain calm. "Can't say that I have."

Larke jerked her head up, staring at him, her eyes bleary with uncertainty. Remaining quiet, she tried to brush past McNair. Before Chase could take another step, the other man reached out, clamping his hand around her wrist. "Not so fast. See, my buddy and I ain't ready for you to leave just yet."

She peered up at him, her eyes wide with fear. His blood turned to ice. It wasn't just McNair who had her scared. She was afraid of him too, unsure how he'd treat her when in the presence of his own kind. Chase shifted his gaze from her, ignoring the searing pain of the knife blade twisting inside him again. Always, when it came to Larke.

"Get your hands off her."

"Don't worry, man. I'll wash my hands later."

"No," Chase bit out, his tone chilly. "You don't understand." He pointed a finger at McNair as he stormed over to them. "*You* need to get *your* nasty hands off her. Not the other way around."

McNair went still. His eyes bulged and his lips curved into an ugly grin. Nodding slowly, he loosened his grip on Larke's wrist, his gaze switching back and forth between them.

A long moment passed before McNair shook his head. He gestured at Larke with his thumb. "This your girl, Hudson? Was she waiting on you? Is that why she's in here?" Chase clenched his jaw, allowing the man to finish his rant while taking note of Larke rubbing her wrist.

McNair gaped at him then let out a harsh chuckle. "Well fuck me. This *is* your goddamn female."

Chase marched right up in his face, snarling at the shorter man. "She's not a *this*. Her name isn't any of your business, either. All *you* need to know is, she's mine and there's not a goddamn thing you, Trevor or anyone else can do about it." He narrowed his eyes on McNair. "Matter of fact, that look on your face got me wondering if you're disappointed I didn't choose you. Are you a jealous, cunt? No? Then stop acting like one and move the fuck on without worrying about who I'm fucking."

McNair pushed away from him and snorted. "Jealous cunt. That's a good one, Hudson. But tell me, what do you *really* think is gonna happen when everyone finds out our soon-to-be leader, is a nasty, dirty, motherfucking race traitor who's been dipping his dick in an inkwell for God only knows how long." McNair tsked and wagged a finger in the air. "That don't sound too good to me."

The urge to launch himself at McNair and rip out his throat was so strong. Chase was a second shy of doing just that when he felt Larke's hand, gently touching him. "Please don't, someone might come." She said this softly, for his ears only.

He clenched his teeth, never taking his eyes off the other man. "Go back to the car," he ordered her. She stared at him in confusion as Chase continued. "I want you to go outside, drive home and wait for me. I'll come soon. Don't worry." *Trust me.*

She wrinkled her brows then gave a firm nod, looking over her shoulder while heading for the exit.

McNair whistled low. "Got that bitch trained too, huh?"

Chase zeroed in on the man he'd despised since childhood. "Shut your goddamn trap for a minute and answer me this. This time try to use your head before you open your mouth again. On a scale of one to ten, how dumb do you think I am?"

McNair curled his lips and sneered, "What the hell that got to do with you and your negro mistress? Or what's gonna happen to you *and* the bitch when I let everyone know."

Chase stepped up in McNair's face, bearing down on him. "Cut the bullshit. You're not scaring anyone." His tone grew serious. "You see that girl who was in here. I'm gonna be honest with you. I care about her. Enough that I thought I could try and be a better person. That's the only reason we're standing here talking, as opposed to my fist down your throat. You remember the last time. So right now, you got two choices. You're gonna keep your mouth real quiet about me and my girl until I'm goddamn good and ready to let everyone know. Or, we're gonna discuss why you've suddenly developed a craving for tacos and burritos, when you can barely stand to look at a fucking Mexican."

McNair snorted, no longer meeting his eyes. "I don't know what you're getting at. Not like you, Hudson. If the color ain't white…"

Chase despised that saying now. He'd heard it too many times over the years and wanted to wipe McNair's mouth clean of it. Leaning in, he bared his teeth. "That's right, you're not like me. But if I were *you*, I'd keep a closer eye on my little Jew princess. All that nice white skin you love so much, working in her daddy's taco restaurant. Things could get *really* messy…"

McNair paled and his jaws ticked as Chase moved away from his long-time nemesis. Now it was all out. They were both race traitors. Only difference between them was, Chase had known for weeks about McNair's Jewish girlfriend, but not once had he thought about confronting or revealing their relationship. McNair on the other would've blackmailed him if he could. So much for white solidarity.

"How'd you find out?" McNair fearfully asked.

"Curiosity and by accident. Just thought to see what was so special about a taco joint that would make someone like you keep going back so often. I pulled up, saw you and a chick with clothes all messed up getting out of your car." Chase shrugged. "I went inside, noticed a picture of her and her dad on the wall. And the name. End of story."

"You didn't tell anyone?"

Chase shook his head. "No. Figured it wasn't my call. Not really anyone's place to tell someone who they can be with, now is it?"

McNair's shoulders slumped. "I don't know, man. There's a lot of things I'm not sure about. I didn't plan on Abigail coming into my life. I saw her one day and couldn't stop myself I guess. Didn't seem to matter that much when I found out she was Jewish. I mean I couldn't press a button and stop liking her." He rubbed his mouth over and over. "I don't know what I'm gonna do. Says she can't introduce me to her parents until I can prove I'm not racist anymore." He stared at Chase. "How the hell am I supposed to turn it off that easily? I haven't touch meth or even alcohol in a while, but how do I stop being racist? Have you figured out how, Hudson?" McNair shook his head hard. "Shit. I can't believe I'm sitting here bitching to you about this."

"You're talking," Chase said. "All I'm doing is listening. I don't have any answers for you. I'm still trying to figure this all out for myself."

"Yeah. Guess I owe you thanks for not saying anything all this time. Thanks. Anyway, I'm sorry for acting like a douche. I shouldn't have put my hand on your girl. Wrong move."

Chase gave a curt nod. "Accepted. Don't let anything like this happen again."

"It won't." McNair touched his nose, which leaned to the side. "Then again, maybe if I do you'll knock my nose back in place." He laughed at his own joke then sobered. "No. Anyway, Hudson. You ever think about leaving? Packing your shit and disappearing into the night. Starting over."

The idea was catching on. "No one's stopping you. Why don't you go for it?"

McNair looked up at him. "What about yourself, since you make it sound so easy. You plan on walking away? Starting over somewhere far away with your girl?"

Alaska didn't sound too bad. Him and Larke, away from it all, surrounded by nature. No one to bother them. "That's none of your business," Chase said. "When and if that happens you'll find out like everybody else." He turned to leave, casting McNair an icy glare. "Remember our talk if you ever think of mentioning my girl to anyone. Jews then blacks…"

Chase left the store then, satisfied at the way McNair had gripped the wall, at the not so subtle reminder of their hierarchy of hate.

Chapter Seventeen

Where is he? Larke paced her apartment for almost an hour. She crossed to the window, looking out for any sign of Chase's red pickup. Maybe she shouldn't have been so quick to follow his command and go home. But his eyes had pleaded, begged her to trust him. She had to.

Inside the store, she'd faltered, believing for a while that he might forsake her in order to save face with a fellow white supremacist. He hadn't. He'd stood up for her even though it meant trouble for him. How much? That's what had her so shaky.

As she made the decision that if after five minutes he didn't show up, she would ring his phone, Larke jumped at the distinct knock on the door. She hurried across the room and peeked out of the peephole. Chase. The heavy of weight of worry dissipated from her shoulders. She drew the door open, throwing herself into his arms before he had a chance to step inside.

"You had me so worried!"

"I'm sorry I took so long. McNair and I needed to get a few things straight." He looked her up and down, and then checked her wrist, smoothing the spot where his "buddy" had grabbed her. "He didn't really hurt you, did he?"

Larke shook her head. "No. I never expected something like

that to happen. Much less inside a store in the middle of the day." She inched away from him and took a deep breath. "I don't like knowing this is some sort of friend of yours."

"McNair and I ain't buddies or friends. We got this thing settled, but that doesn't mean we're cool or that I trust him. You're my only friend. The only person I trust." Chase raked a hand through his hair. "Anyways, I'm real sorry that happened. I knew the fucker was a hunter but there's no way I could've known he'd be in there today."

"It wasn't your fault. What happened after I left?"

"We talked."

She frowned. "Talked? He didn't strike me as the type of person anyone could talk things out with."

Chase strode across the room, taking a seat on the couch. "Maybe not. He was willing to listen this time. So, it's all good. Everything is fine." He tapped the cushion next to him. "Come sit beside me."

Larked folded her arms. How could he be so casual about what just happened? She refused to move from her spot. Eyeing him carefully, she asked, "So, you're not concerned at all about everyone knowing you're in a relationship with me?"

"Didn't I just tell you everything was settled? McNair won't open his mouth. He has too much to lose."

"Like you? Do you also have too much to lose because of me?"

Chase stared at her for what felt like an eternity without saying a word. Larke watched as he glanced down at his hand then slowly brought his attention to her. "I do have a lot to lose," he began. "Nothing I'm scared of losing, though. You just gotta understand it ain't that easy shedding years of well...everything I am. Was. I don't really care what people say. You know me, Larke. But I won't lie and tell you it'll be a walk in the park when every single member of Antebellum Resistance finds out I'm a race traitor. I never heard of anyone doing anything like that before, especially not while living in our community."

Larke sat beside him, humbled at his honesty and hating the path his family had laid out for him. The situation could've easily been reversed if her parents had been the fanatics. She laced her arm around his shoulder. "Do you worry they'll try to…" God, she couldn't even bring herself to finish the terrifying sentence.

He shook his head. "No. There's a bunch of hotheads, like McNair for instance and some actual nutjobs, who've already gotten themselves locked up a time or two. The majority are just pissed at life. I never saw it before. But I get it now. They think the government and life in general abandoned them. Take that sinkhole we fell into. You know what caused it?"

She shook her head. "Tell me."

"The whole area used to be a mining town. They used to drill mining tunnels across the woodlands. After a while the ground just caved in and that's what caused it. When the mine closed, lots of people got real frustrated. My grandfather was able to buy up most of that land dirt cheap back then, cause the town was dead. The first few members he recruited were starving miners. He got them to help him build up the town with a promise of a better future. For whites. Since they were the ones suffering. That's how all this mess got started. And it just grew and grew and sucked us all in."

Jesus. And now she was sucked in too, Larke thought. "Did your grandfather tell you all of this before he died?"

Chase curled his lips and chuckled harshly. "Bits and pieces. He sounded like a big hero when he told it. The rest I figured out on my own."

"It's sad isn't it? The fact that race traitor is even a term although there's nothing traitorous about two people wanting to be together. Yesterday, I thought about it also. I thought maybe race traitor applied to me but in a different way. The only difference is, not once did I draw any conclusion that us being together was wrong.

Do you still think it is, not you and me, but in general for other people?"

"I don't." He looked down at her hand on his. "You see that I'm trying real hard, don't you? Like I promised. I don't even wanna think some of those words I used to use before. They don't feel right and makes me think about you being all sad and hurt. Sometimes, I *do* have to try extra hard to watch what I say because it might be wrong." He ran his thumb along her nape.

Larke bit her lip, becoming aroused as he kept talking. "Like I've been wanting to tell you how pretty your skin is. When I saw you naked for the first time all I could think about was touching and tasting you all over. It really did remind me of chocolate, but I figured I shouldn't say stuff like that. Right?"

The pulse in the base of her neck began to beat hard and rapidly. "It's not the best thing to say, but it's not bad." Larke leaned into him as his lips caressed her neck. "The way you put it though, I almost wished I did taste like that."

Chase raised his head and murmured close to her ear, "You taste much better. I told you so remember—said you tasted better than candy. I meant chocolate but didn't want to outright say it."

She laughed softly, suddenly recalling those very words and the warm feel of his tongue against her clit two nights ago. She drew her legs together, feeling moisture gathering at her core. "I love all the things we've done together. Sometimes I even lie awake in bed with my eyes closed picturing it all."

He drew his gaze to her thighs, held pressed together. Lifting his head, he captured her stare.

"Don't do that."

"Don't do what?"

"Squeeze your legs together like that. You've got an ache and what you're doing isn't gonna make it go away."

"What do you suggest?" Larke asked huskily.

"Me. When I'm here I'll take care of you. When I'm not here

and you can't wait, then I want you to slip your fingers inside and play with yourself real nice. Think about how I'll reward you with my dick the next time, if you make yourself come.

"R-reward me?" she stuttered, splaying her thighs for him now.

Chase tipped her chin. "Yes. I also need to do so for how well you listened to me in the hunting store earlier. You made me proud."

"Will you reward me now?" she breathed. Her mind was already conjuring the most erotic images of Chase on top of her, behind her. Everywhere. Larke sighed inside her head, anticipating the bliss to come.

He knelt in front of her and peeled down her panties from beneath her dress. He nuzzled his face between her breasts. Soon after, Chase drew his head up and relaxed into the couch, leaning back to open his pants.

Larke groaned as his cock sprang forward, massive and thick, the engorged tip curving upward. Holding her by the hips, he said, "Come sit on my dick."

Oh my God. She almost spluttered in shock. In all the time, the many times they'd made love, it was always Chase who well... penetrated her. Larke bit her lip then shook her head slowly, despite her pussy clenching and quivering with excitement. If he really meant for her to just sink, impale herself on him... Jesus. Yet, as she heard herself whisper, "I can't," her legs were already moving toward him, brushing against his pants.

Chase ran his hand along the veiny base. "I wasn't asking if you could. Was more like an order. We're long past games and you being scared. You ain't a virgin anymore, Larke. I've been fucking and coming inside you a lot, so it shouldn't hurt." He looked down and groaned as she rubbed the pad of her thumb over the glistening tip. "I gotta get you used to taking me how I want it. Right now, I need you to sit right here on top of me so I can watch the look on your face when you take me all the way in."

Her entire body shivered. Holding on to his shoulders, Larke straddled his waist and inhaled through her nose as she lowered her wetness over the heated crown.

Breath left her body. She was completely filled. Larke cried out then moaned because impossible as it was, it felt as if his penis went all the way up to her belly. She scratched her fingernails against his back, shutting her eyes in abandon when her walls closed around him.

Chase gave her a languid grin while one hand went beneath her dress and up, stroking her breast. "Angel, you're so snug. Squeezing all around me."

In response, Larke undulated her hips, bouncing on his rock hard shaft. The smile on his lips melted as he growled, "Yes!" He grabbed her by the hips compelling her to ride him hard. Before Larke could form another thought, Chase rose from the couch. Gasping, she locked her legs around his waist, ankles crossed at his back as he crossed the room and pinned her to an adjoining wall.

"Only so much I can take," he grunted, before pulling out almost completely then shoving into her in one powerful thrust, causing her to cry out in shock and pleasure.

"Can barely sleep at night thinking about you. About *this*." He held her trapped under his gaze and pressed to the wall, impaled by his cock. "Did you think I was going to leave you in control?"

She whimpered, struggling to form a coherent sentence. "Chase. Please. I can't think."

He drove into her harder than before with one hand holding her against the waist the other wrapped in her braids. "Tell me who you belong to."

"You," she breathed, moaning softly. "I belong to you."

He growled his approval. "Not good enough. Tell me no matter what happens, you won't ever leave me."

Oh God! Larke sucked in a breath as her mind spun trying to concentrate on his demand. He sensed her hesitation, withdrew then pushed forward like a piston at full throttle, ramming into her with one savage thrust after the other, wringing hoarse cries from the back of her throat. Without warning his movements slowed to an agonizingly sweet tempo that sent shivers racing across her skin. "I need this from you, Larke. I know it's asking a lot, but I need this so bad. I need to know that no matter what, I can always come to you. I can always come back to this, fucking my girl until everything feels right inside my messed up world."

Tears burned at the back of her lids. Chase's plea threatened to unravel her. "I won't leave you. I promise I won't."

"Good," he whispered. "You're my home, angel. Right here, deep inside you is the only place I feel at home. I love you." He pressed his forehead to hers, shaking his head as he continued to thrust into her pussy. Frozen into shock, Larke realized he hadn't meant to say the words that were now causing her heart to leap and slam against her ribcage like the beating of a thousand drums.

"Chase." She clasped her arms around him tighter as he nuzzled the side of her neck with his lips. "I don't know when it happened," he continued huskily. "I just know that I love you so much and I can't stop. I know you don't love me but that's fine." He crushed his lips over hers and upped his tempo, fucking her hard and fast. "I'm good with this for now. Having you all to myself. Coming inside you and feeling you come all around me."

Larke sank her teeth into her lip, her entire body shuddering, her breath coming in ragged pants at the same time her body gave in to the heart stopping pleasure shooting out from deep inside. Lost in ecstasy, she sighed against his shoulder as he threw his head back, climaxing alongside her.

Chase released her, gently setting her on her feet. He wasn't done, however. With one hand splayed against the wall above her head, he remained unmoving, blocking her path. Trapped. If it were anyone else she would have viewed it as a threatening stance. Not him. If anything, she felt her lower belly heat under his intense stare. "You're not mad at me cause of what I said, are you?" he asked, features hard. Vulnerable.

"You said a lot of things," she said softly, meeting his eyes.

"I mean about loving you. I didn't plan on telling you yet, but seeing you there... The way I was feeling. I couldn't hold it in. I didn't mean to put you on the spot. Wasn't my intention at all."

"You didn't. I'm glad you told me." Larke touched his face, tracing her fingers across his lips. "I—"

"It's okay." Chase cut her off. "You don't have to say anything back." He dropped his hand from the wall, righting his pants as he strode away from her.

In that moment, Larke despised herself. He'd noticed her brief hesitation.

"I didn't hurt you, did I?" He was watching her slide her panties back on.

She shook her head. "You didn't." *But I hurt you.* Yes. She was the one who had done the hurting today. Regret gnawed at her. She should've told him. She should've given in without fear and hesitation and told Chase how much she loved him too. But it was too late now. Her credibility was shot. He would think she was saying it out of guilt and pity. Chase hated pity.

Sighing inwardly, she asked, "You don't have to go soon, do you?"

"There's no one waiting on me."

"What about your stepfather?" Larke asked, selfishly contemplating what the man's death would mean for Chase and the group. "How is he doing?"

Chase lifted a shoulder. "I saw him earlier before you called me. He's gotten worse. Guess his time is coming up real soon."

"Oh."

He nodded, although his features now appeared closed. Guarded somewhat. *Because of her?*

Her heart twisted. But then Larke recalled something she'd wanted to ask him. If Chase saw that she wanted him to meet her friends maybe it would help somewhat to *show* him how much he meant to her, before she confessed her love for him. Bolstered by the idea, she asked, "Have you ever gone bowling?"

His eyes widened, regarding her as if she'd lost her mind. "You mean that place I saw you getting your ass slapped?"

She glared. "Thanks for reminding me. But yes *and* from the look on your face I'd say it's a no go." She gazed at him, hoping he'd prove her wrong by agreeing to go.

"Why?" His brows furrowed. With suspicion?

"I thought it might be fun. And I could introduce you to my friend and her boyfriend."

"The Indian girl you went to nursing school with and her black teacher boyfriend?"

Larke frowned, somehow troubled at his tone of voice and well, that he had to mention those details, as if they bothered him.

"That's them," she answered. "Riva and Jason. We could do a couple of rounds and leave if we're not having fun. There's an alley not too far from here so I don't think we'll have another incident like the one inside the hunting store."

"Did you tell your friends about me?"

"I told Riva. She suspected I was seeing someone. I trust her. But even if I hadn't said anything, they would've remembered you."

"They won't mind me being there?"

"They won't. I wouldn't have mentioned it if they did."

Chase's eyes grew colder by the second. Distant. "I think I'll pass."

"Why? Do you have other plans?" she asked, slightly afraid it was about him not wishing to be around other races.

He read the worry on her face and snapped, "Stop trying to read my mind." He started pacing the living room, paused, then spun around, facing her. "Look. I know you always try to see the good in everyone and stay positive, which is a good thing, or else you wouldn't be with me. But c'mon, Larke, you don't really believe your friends actually want to hang out with me unless they wanna use it as an opportunity to talk down and preach to me. The ignorant, redneck, racist asshole. I might not be as smart as you and your friends, but I know how this works."

Her stomach dropped. Chase thought she would invite him out so her friends could ridicule him? She stared at him in disbelief. He couldn't. He honestly couldn't. And she refused to believe he did. He knew her, had to know by now, that she'd never let anyone mistreat him in front of her.

Larke carefully chose her next words. "Other people might think they know you, similar to how I was so sure I knew everything about you in the beginning. But they don't. They don't see you the way I do and there's no way I would sit back and let anyone talk down to you or say awful things to you. Just like I know you wouldn't do the same to them."

He said nothing although the tell tale signs of frustration and anger were gone. Larke decided to push her luck. "You mentioned my friends being more intelligent than you. I don't believe in comparing intelligence, but have you noticed that lately a lot of your actions haven't been that of a die-hard white supremacist? Isn't it blasphemy to suggest a person of color being smarter than you? When you saw that little boy chasing after his dog, you never hesitated to help. And don't think I missed the way you looked at him when you spoke. There wasn't a shred of prejudice in your eyes. Those things tell me a lot."

Chase shrugged. "Maybe it just means I suck really bad at being a die hard racist."

She reached for his hand. "I'm waiting on the day you completely fail at it."

He chuckled low, without humor. "Trying my best, angel."

Chapter Eighteen

His girlfriend was insane. That was the conclusion Chase came to after Larke begged, no ordered him over the phone to clear a day in the week, but not a weekend, for her completely. That was fair enough and he'd been happy to do it. The insane part came after he'd driven to her place, found her dressed and waiting beside her car.

She tapped her watch then scolded. "I thought you said you'd be here at nine. It's nine-ten."

He stared at her, baffled until she started laughing and kissed his lips. "Chase, I'm joking. Actually, it's the opposite. Today we won't worry about time."

"We won't?"

She shook her head and beamed, gazing up at him as if she was in lo… He shook the thought away before it could take root. "Nope," she said, "I've put myself in charge and I'm kidnapping you for the day." She walked to the passenger side of her car and held the door open. "Get in."

His lips twitched. "Just like that?"

"Just like that," she repeated. Shaking his head, Chase did as ordered. He blinked in surprise as she closed the door for him.

Soon, Larke was seated behind the steering wheel, looking over at him. "Are you scared?" She wrinkled her brows to appear terrifying.

He leaned over and kissed her, unable to resist the urge. "A little, yeah."

She laughed as they drove down the street, merging into the lane for the highway.

"Where are we going?"

"It's a surprise. You know that."

"Surprises aren't always good, angel. At least give me a hint."

She glanced at him, her eyes soft and said quietly, "With me they are."

He said nothing to that, mostly because his throat was starting to feel thick again from that look she'd just given him. A look that made him wish more than anything, that he was right in thinking, maybe Larke loved him as much as he loved her.

She quirked her lips and flashed him a grin. "Okay. I'll give you this hint. There'll probably be a lot of people there. It's wide and open. Lots of fun,

Larke had him stumped. Shrugging, he sank back in the seat. "All right. I'm all yours."

She glanced over at him with a shy smile and whispered, "I'm all yours, too."

His heart slammed against his chest as he continued to watch her while she drove. About half an hour later, Chase realized exactly what Larke had in mind. An amusement park. Fuck. She was taking him to an amusement park.

He drew up in the seat, minutes after and turned to her. "This is cause of that bowling alley thing, isn't it?"

She parked and killed the engine. "Of course it is."

Chase pinched the bridge of his nose. Larke was staring at him, excited, appearing pleased with herself and he was being an ass.

Ungrateful. Taking a deep breath he asked, "Why here? We could've gone bowling, just the two of us if it meant that much to you."

"Going bowling doesn't mean anything to me. I only wanted to do something fun with you. Silly fun. The kind I know you didn't have growing up."

"What about your friends? I thought you wanted me to meet them."

"I did. I still do. But we have time." She looked at him and laughed, although it didn't quite reach her eyes as it usually did. "Maybe one day I'll even get to meet some of your friends." She stopped laughing and gave a fake cough. "That was a joke. A bad one. I'm not stupid."

No. Larke wasn't stupid. She was hurting, though. Deep inside and even a beast like him could tell. "It won't always be like this," he said quietly, needing to reassure her some way.

"I know." She placed her hand in his. "I know you'll do right by us."

I will, angel. I will.

Wanting to lighten the mood, Chase raised his brows and cocked his head toward the amusement park's entrance. "You come here a lot, Larke? Brought lots of guys?"

She laughed loud. This time, the smile reached her eyes, making them appear to sparkle. "Way too many to count. But…if you must know. There's a reason I brought you here and not just anywhere else. More than one reason."

"I'm listening."

"Remember when I told you how I wanted to do things other kids were able to do? Well this place helped. This was the school trip I had really wanted to go on. The reason I sucked up my fear and found a way to cope. She looked over at him and pursed her lips. "The other reason is…" Larke sighed loudly. "I don't want to offend you, but from everything you've told me, it sounds as if you've had a pretty horrible childhood. I don't pity you, Chase but

I don't see anything wrong with us spending the day together, not being so *adult*." She raised one brow. "What do you say? My treat. All day long."

His throat tightened. "Sounds good," he said, trying to act normal when all he wanted to do was take her in his arms, bury his face in her neck and never let up.

Once inside it was plain to see the amusement park was much bigger than it seemed from the outside. Then again, he'd didn't know what he'd really expected since he had never been to one before. It was also packed despite being a weekday. Now he understood why Larke didn't want them to go on a weekend.

Strolling hand in hand they made their way through a throng of people and nearing a play area with sprinklers and water fountains. Chase noticed Larke staring at the toddlers running around giggling and screaming, each time the water sprayed up and hit them.

Did she like children? She had to, he guessed, if she wrote books for them. He stared at her again as her smile widened. Chase doubted she even realized what she was doing. But he couldn't stop his mind from wandering. Him and Larke were going to be together forever, if things went the way he wanted. The way he hoped they would after he proved to her that he really was a changed man, despite what he'd told her weeks ago.

Let Larke see how much he wanted a life with her. Her alone. And one that included giving her all the children she wanted. Because from the way her eyes softened at the sight of those kids, he was almost sure she'd want a bunch. His cock twitched and his balls drew up as his gaze washed over her. Chase was already picturing her curvy body filling out, growing rounder, with her breasts so damn ripe and belly swollen with his kid.

Damn.

His mouth went dry as he watched her again, struck by how even in the middle of an amusement park he was thinking about being intimate with her. Chase sucked in a breath, burying those thoughts for now. He held her close, glad she had chosen this place to bring him. Allowing him to be around people being so *normal*. To *feel* normal.

Larke clutched her stomach while eyeing the roller coaster they'd ridden minutes ago. She glared at Chase, knowing he'd chosen it as payback because she'd dragged him into the drop tower ride. Although her heart had been inside her throat, she'd almost burst out laughing at the muffled expletive he'd muttered when the gondola dropped without warning.

"This is what you like?" he'd asked, gaping at her in awe and horror once they'd left that ride.

Her ensuing laughter had prompted Chase to glance at the monstrous roller coaster that dominated the backdrop of the park and declare it their next stop. Slightly nauseous, she held on to Chase's hand while scowling at the smug grin on his face. Behind the scowl, however, Larke was beyond happy that he was enjoying this silly gift of hers.

After riding the majority of the attractions, they exited the park as more and more people trickled in. She turned to Chase who had two cheesy teddy bears in his hand, which he'd won for her in a game of darts. He placed the bears on the backseat of the car.

"Ready for round two?" she asked, standing beside him in the parking lot.

He arched an eyebrow. "As long as it doesn't involve any more thrill rides."

"You forced me on that roller coaster. You don't get any sympathy from me."

He grinned and stepped in front of her, grazing his knuckles across her cheek. "Sympathy ain't what I want from you, Larke. But if you're mad at me you can always let me make it up to you real good tonight."

She swept her tongue across her lip. "How good?"

"The—I haven't been inside my girl for two days and that's way too long for me—type of good. Can't get enough of you because of how much I love you and the way you treat me."

Her breath hitched, moisture seeped into her panties. But most of all, her heart thumped wildly inside her chest, bursting with love for him. "I'm not opposed to any of that," she whispered, reaching up on her toes to kiss him.

She moaned softly as Chase's large hand cupped the back of her head, kissing her hard. They both pulled back, drawing in air. Larke found her voice, shaky as it was. "Come on, let's go."

"You want me to drive?"

"No. I'm in charge today, remember?" She flashed him a grin then went around to the driver's side.

Larke loved the look on his face when they got out. Surprise then a slow shake of his head followed by a small grin. "You're really giving me the treatment today huh, angel?"

"I sure am. I figured this would be another place you'd never been or come to as a grown man."

He nodded. "You're right on both counts."

They were at an ice cream parlor. Ridiculous as it might seem taking a card-carrying white supremacist out for frozen treats, it actually *wasn't*. Today she had once again witnessed Chase showing the side of him that was straying farther and farther away from his long-held beliefs. Caught in a rush of people walking by, a man clearly Hispanic and brown, though much lighter than herself had accidentally bumped into Chase. For a brief moment Larke had kept her breath held, half afraid of how Chase would react.

He'd nodded at the man's apology, assuring the man it was fine. Larke hadn't said anything because she hadn't wanted him to feel awkward. Instead, they'd continued along as if nothing had happened. And so in her mind, that was also a good reason to sit down for ice cream with the man she adored. Adored *and* admired for attempting to become a better person.

Inside, Larke sat across from Chase and flipped through the menu. It took less than five seconds to know what she wanted. Double Chocolate Sundae with whipped cream topping.

"That was fast." He glanced up at her from his menu. "You recommend anything?"

Larke showed him some of her favorite flavors and was glad when he settled on the Peanut Vanilla and Chocolate Sundae after the waiter came to take their order.

Chase leaned forward in his chair and gave her a lazy grin that made her heart flip. *I love him so much.*

And she would tell him soon. When she did, it would be so perfect because he wouldn't think she was repeating the words to make him feel good. Chase would understand and *know* how much she loved him and how proud she was of the changes he'd made. Changes Larke wasn't sure he even realized he'd made.

"Would you really wanna see my house?"

She blinked and frowned. "The lake house?"

"No." He shook his head. "Where I live, angel. Lee's Fortress."

Oh. She forced herself to sound calmer than she felt. "I'd like to at some point. But I know how complicated that would be. I don't want you to have any problems because of me. I can wait until…"

He nodded. Understanding what her silence meant. Until he left the group. Until he turned his back on the life of a white suprem-acist. But even then, her going to his home would be iffy. The people living there would *still* hate her, even more so for encouraging him to leave. Larke sighed as Chase gazed back at her, his eyes troubled.

She was grateful when the waiter suddenly appeared with their ice cream, breaking the heavy moment.

Watching him push back the sleeve of his shirt and dip the long spoon into the sundae, Larke became curious, asking, "Was it just you or were all the kids who grew up in your community restricted from doing " Air quotes. "Normal stuff. Television watching, going out to eat, fun kid stuff?"

Chase pressed his thumb to his lips, thoughtful. "I can't speak for everyone. But most of the kids I knew didn't have a TV in their house. That's normal. Lots of fear of brainwashing. Truthfully, since I started watching television, I can see where the fear comes from. Not saying it's right, just that I get it. I *understand* why they thought we'd be influenced." He shrugged. "How it is."

"I've thought about something else," she said. "You mentioned that you were homeschooled. But what happened after your mother left? Did you end up going to a regular school?"

He shook his head. "Most of the other kids were homeschooled and the everyone always tried to keep it as legit as possible so the state wouldn't come snooping around. I taught myself and did most of the work I needed to get done. I gotta admit though, after a while I got tired of school and stopped altogether. Figured I'd be better off working; then I wouldn't ever have to depend on anyone for anything.

"When did you stop?"

"Sixteen. I probably could have stopped earlier cause it didn't look like anyone was checking up on us, anyway." He stared at her and arched a brow. "Just because I'm not educated like you, doesn't mean I'm nothing. I mean, it's not that bad talking to me, right?"

Larke swallowed the lump in her throat and blinked away a tear before he could see it. "I *never* thought that. Not once. Chase, if anyone ever said that to you, then they're obviously wrong. Being book smart doesn't tell the whole story of a person. And it's also not a standard for intelligence. Plus, none of that matters to me. You're all that matters. You mean more to me than anyone else and I love talking to you."

He gave her a boyish grin. "Could it also be that you like talking to me because you do most of the talking anyway?"

She laughed and took a scoop of ice cream. "Could be. But...

if you don't like me talking so much, you could always kiss me to shut me up."

Before Larke could react Chase leaned across the table and did just that; covered her mouth with his.

"I didn't mean now," she whispered afterward.

He relaxed in his chair. "You're my girl, Larke. I can kiss you whenever I want. That ain't something you should forget anytime soon."

Chapter Nineteen

"I am *done*," Chase said to himself as he entered his house. There was no way he could continue as before. Yesterday had been so perfect—Larke surprising him with that amazing and thoughtful day out. They'd spent that same night talking, laughing and making love until they were both exhausted. The next morning, he'd awoken with her head on his chest. She'd been fast asleep, her body tired and sore from all the ways he'd taken her.

Chase had barely taken off his shoes before his phone began to ring. The caller was Roy Simmons, one of Trevor's underlings. The accountant. He ignored it. His stepfather had probably convinced the man to call for some reason or the other because he was too ill to do it himself. *Too fucking bad.*

Since the start of the week, Trevor's condition had taken a turn for the worse. He was laid up in bed, unable to do so much as use the bathroom on his own and was under the constant care of a nurse. Chase curled his lip, half anticipating and half dreading his planned visit to the older man. It was going be ugly watching someone in Trevor's condition, a man about to die and meet his Maker, try and tell Chase his relationship with Larke was wrong.

"Wrong is laughing after you watch someone pump a bullet

into an innocent person's brain," he muttered out loud. "Wrong was me keeping my damn mouth shut for so long, even if I was a kid and had nothing to do with it." Chase crossed the living room, stopping short as his gaze landed and zeroed in on a spot on the wall. It was an old picture; one that had hung there since before he'd learned to walk. This was the same picture he'd walked by every single day of his life without giving a second thought. *Shameful.*

Anger steamed and seethed inside Chase's blood as he stalked toward the picture. Ripping it from the wall, he stared...glared at it. Disgust for himself and his entire family, burned inside of him. Because in the photo staring back at him was his grandfather. Appearing only a few years older than Chase, Joseph stood proud and tall in his finest white robes, surrounded by some of his closest friends. They were all dressed in white. Without their hoods.

Chase closed his eyes and recognized the tormented growl ripping across the room as his own. Bile rose and seared like acid from within his gut to the base of his throat. Images of the reporter he'd witnessed his grandfather shooting, assailed him. The sound of the bullet splitting the man's skull. So much blood splattering all over the wall. Blood *he'd* had to help clean up.

Hurling the photo across the room, Chase clutched his head, fighting against the pain as memory after memory bombarded him. His grandfather had laughed alongside Trevor while the Chinese man lay dying on the floor. How many sick things had they done before? Chase had never allowed himself to really go that deep, questioning the violence surrounding his family's twisted beliefs. But now it was inside his head and wasn't going anywhere. Just like his love for Larke, which *definitely* wasn't going away anytime now or in the future.

Larke.

Her gorgeous round face. Smiling at him, looking at him all the time as if he was someone special.

Lips parted, crying for me to come deep inside her.

His body shuddered. Images of his grandfather and Larke

collided. If the old man was still alive, would he have tried to hurt her? Laugh while watching the woman Chase loved suffer at his hands?

"No," he shouted then lowered his voice, whispering to himself. "I wouldn't have let him hurt her." He would've killed Joseph Butler himself before allowing the old racist to put his filthy hands on Larke.

Sickened, Chase jumped in his pickup and drove the short distance to Trevor's house. He knocked despite having a key, simply because he didn't want the nurse to freak out, assuming someone was breaking in. The young redheaded woman opened the door and greeted him. "Mr. Douglas is inside his room resting, should I let him know you're here?"

"I can see myself in." Chase bypassed the nurse and entered Trevor's room.

His stepfather, ill as he was didn't bother attempting to sit up. His jaundiced gaze connected with Chase as a bout of coughing racked his frail body. "That bitch out there won't give me my cigarettes," Trevor croaked. "Can you believe that?"

Chase pulled up a chair at his bedside. "I believe it. She's doing her job. I don't know why you like that shit so much. It's what got you here."

Trevor rolled his eyes. When he spoke, his voice was barely audible. "Keep the goddamn lecture to yourself, boy. What do you want anyway?"

"To talk."

"Do I look like I'm up for a chat?" He scowled as if Chase had lost his damn mind. He hadn't. Had finally found it.

Chase leaned forward, pitying the man lying on the bed. His hair was stringy and in patches. His face sullen, eyes almost sunken in. With every breath Chase inhaled, he could smell the musty odor of illness and other things he didn't even want to think about. "Humor me, Trevor. For the last time. I just wanna ask you something."

"Ask your fucking question," Trevor wheezed. "Laid up here can hardly catch a damn breath and you wanna have a tea party."

Ignoring his stepfather grumblings, Chase said, "You and Joe always taught me that it was Jewish people controlling the media. Manipulating people into thinking race mixing is okay. Is that right or is there another explanation, like two people genuinely wanting to be together because they can't stand to be apart?"

Trevor slanted his head toward Chase, giving him the side-eye. "Jewish people," he mimicked. "Since when you get so goddamn PC?"

"Just answer the question."

"Of course it's Jew brainwashing. Why else you think that shit doesn't affect us? No TV, no bullshit propaganda."

"Hmm." Chase folded his arms, staring straight ahead. "See, Trev, I can't buy into that kind of reasoning anymore because I've finally got a girl."

Trevor watched him, his brows drawn and his feature taut, as if he sensed a storm. Chase scratched his chin and smiled despite Trevor's glare. "She's not like any other girl I know. For starters, she's black. Also the kindest person I've ever met and the cutest girl I know. See, this is also gonna piss you off, but my girl is smarter than everyone in Lee's Fortress put together. I'm in love. I'm not alone anymore and I can't seem to give a fuck what you or anyone else has to say about it."

Trevor's breathing grew harsh, a low wheeze thrumming into the now silent room. His eyes remained wide with a look of pure hatred directed at Chase. His lips were drawn into a tight line with bits of froth foaming around the corner. A long moment passed until Trevor opened his mouth, slowly as if it caused him great physical pain to do so. More than before. "Fucking traitor. Joe should've..." He wheezed again. "Shot. Your ass. Long..." Cough. "Time ago."

Chase stood, unaffected by what he heard. "Too late for that." He brought his hands together. "Anyway, since we both hate small talks, I'm heading on out of here. That was all I came for. Oh and to let you know, I'm tired of hating people for reasons that don't make sense. I'm done."

"AR?" Trevor wheezed hard. "Quitting for your *negress?*"

The muscles in Chase's jaws clenched. He glowered, knowing the dying man was trying to incite a reaction from him. "I am. For her. For myself. I ain't leading a bunch of racists, let somebody else do it."

The froth around Trevor's lips thickened as he struggled to open his mouth. By the time he did, Chase was already to the door, no longer listening. The nurse was seated on the couch in the living room, filling out a sheet of paper.

"You should probably have a look at him," Chase told her. "He's foaming at the mouth. Think he's really pissed about not getting those cigarettes." He vaguely took notice of the nurse pushing the paper away then dashing across the living room as he walked out the door.

Chase looked back at the house while pulling out of the driveway. Despite knowing he'd soon have to deal with arranging his stepfather's funeral, since he doubted the man would live out the rest of the month, much less the week, he felt lighter. He felt proud. He'd done it. The truth about him and Larke was out and he couldn't be happier. From now on, it would be only him and her. Nothing or no one in between.

Some time later as Chase was seated around his table, going over required documents for the cargo ship, he was interrupted by a sharp knock on the door. Through the window, he recognized the car outside as belonging to Roy Simmons.

"What do you want?" Chase asked, annoyed as he drew the door open. After just telling Trevor he was done, the last thing he wanted was to talk business. He was pulling himself out. What went on inside AR no longer concerned him. Roy would learn that soon, like everyone else.

"Can I come in?"

"Yeah, sure." Chase gestured the man inside the house. "I saw your call from this morning."

Roy, with his balding head, stared at him as if he expected Chase to say more. When Chase didn't, he snorted and shook his head. "Right. Anyway. I didn't come over here to see how you're holding up. This is important." Roy showed himself over to the table and plopped his folder on beside Chase's work."

'What's all that for?"

The accountant pinched his forehead then raised his head, looking almost fearful. "You know I've been managing the books for a couple of years."

"Yeah. So?"

"As much as I like Trevor, we both know he's not the easiest person to talk to. That's why I'm coming to you. I couldn't say anything before."

"Say it, man. Whatever it is, just say it. Don't waste my time. You see I was working over here, don't you?" he said, gesturing to his own stack of paperwork.

"We're in trouble."

Chase raised his brows. "We?"

Roy gazed up from the papers he was opening. "Antebellum Resistance. Lee's Fortress. It's all of us. Here take a look for yourself."

Frowning, Chase reluctantly took the papers, reading through them carefully; including the letter from the IRS citing the thousands of dollars in back taxes owed.

Shit. Was that what Trevor had been hinting at when he mentioned money was running low? But where did it all go?

Chase raised his head. Roy must have read the questions on his face because he quickly said. "The money raised from selling AR paraphernalia, from donors, and dues—most of it went toward the monthly stipend we've been handing out."

The one most of the people had come to depend on because they either genuinely couldn't find work—which was the case for a few—or they used the excuse that only minorities were getting work due to government favoritism. Chase shook his head and stared at Roy, wondering if the man didn't realize how their own views were leading to their downfall.

But of course, the handouts had been their great experiment, meant to lure more nationalists or would-be nationalists into joining the movement. And Chase was guilty because he too, had agreed to and thought it was a good idea at the time. He swallowed hard, fighting back shame and regret.

Chase handed back the paperwork . "What do you expect me to do?"

Roy gaped. "Trevor's a breath away from death. You're the one in charge now. Everyone knows that. He even sent outa memo stating you'd be taking over when he dies. You're Joe's grandson, of course you're in charge."

"I don't care." Chase ground his teeth. "Let the IRS take what they want. Being Joe Butler's grandson hasn't made my life any better. Same goes for my relationship with Trevor. As a matter of fact, I don't even wanna hear his fucking name inside my house."

Roy's eyes bulged behind his glasses. "I don't know what happened between you and Tr–him, but you of all people should know it's more than handing property over to the IRS. I'm going to leave all this here and you take some time, not too long. And then tell me, you're out."

Long after the accountant left, Chase sat at the table, staring at the paperwork. He didn't need to read through the rest. He already knew what Roy meant. He closed his eyes and shook his head, torn between laughing and crying like a goddamn kid.

Chase wasn't even sure how he got there, but some time later, he found himself standing in front of Larke's apartment, knocking. The door slowly opened. She stood there with one arm against the wall holding the door ajar. "Back so soon?" Her lips curved into a playful sexy grin. He tried to force a smile but couldn't. "Open the door, Larke."

The smile on her lips froze. She held the door wide, stepping back as he strode inside.

"What happened?"

He drew in a shaky breath then let it out. "What didn't happen you mean. For starters, I think my stepdad might die anytime now."

"Oh. I—"

"You don't have to pretend to feel sorry. I'm not."

"Then what's wrong? You seem so…so. I don't even know. Kind of angry."

"Angry, frustrated. A lot of things to be honest. I went to see him today. Told him about you. About us."

Her face softened. "Oh, Chase. How did he react?"

"Pissed. Think I might have speeded up his death."

"Now that your stepfather knows, I guess soon everyone else will also know that you no longer have those beliefs. That you're not a part of the group anymore."

I'm gonna break her heart. Break my girl's heart so bad.

Chase felt sickened, wanted to vomit. But more so, he wanted to drop to his knees and beg Larke to understand everything he had to say. Maybe she would…

"They won't know that."

She raised her brows. "Why not?"

"Because I can't walk away."

"What?" The raw pain and confusion on her face stabbed into his heart. "Why, Chase? I don't understand. I thought you *wanted* to leave it all behind you."

He headed toward her, backing up as Larke flinched away from him. "I do," he said, praying she'd understand he had no other choice. "But I can't walk away yet. I planned to. I swear to God, I did. Today, before I came here, I found out that a lot of people might suffer if I turn my back so quickly." Embarrassed and ashamed, he told her all about the 'stipend' program and its aim.

"You once told you me that it was the adult's responsibility when I mentioned not having any food as a kid and having to hunt. Well, now it's *my* responsibility because I allowed Trevor to make those people dependent on the handouts.

Larke stubbornly folded her arms and shook her head. "No. I don't accept that reasoning. No one forces anyone to do anything. I understand you not wanting the people to suffer; the children who live there, but why does it have to be you who takes on full responsibility? If they're that impoverished, they can ask the government for help. There are programs out there, they just have to get out of their racist mindset and bubble. And if they're so desperate for someone to lead them, what about that psycho we saw in the hunting store? He seemed fanatical enough."

"There's no one else," Chase shouted, growing frustrated by the second. Why wasn't she getting it? Normally Larke was so sweet and accepting. He had people depending on him. Didn't she understand the guilt he'd feel knowing other children would suffer the way he did as a child?

She stared at him, her eyes shiny. With tears? Fuck. He hadn't wanted this. Chase closed the distance between them, reaching out to hold her. Comfort her from the hurt he was raining down. "Larke, please. You have to trust me. It won't always be like this."

She sidestepped him, pulling away. "I trusted you before. How do you expect me to be with someone who heads a group of people who'd rather see me dead than sit down and have a coffee or friendly talk with me?" Larke shook her head and wiped at her eyes. "I can't do it, Chase. I wish I could, but this is too much."

His mind screamed at her. *It's not too much. You can handle anything. You've handled everything from me so far.*

"I mean, honestly, will I still be able to come over to your house? Will this be the time I get to meet all your friends? Family maybe?" She let out a hurt laugh. "The answer's no, isn't it? I definitely can't tag along to any of your 'gatherings' or meet all these important people, who I suppose you're going to have to meet if you want to get more funds for your precious people. People who need, and *deserve* you much more than I do.

"It ain't like that," he snapped. "For fuck's sake. Just be normal. Accept this."

"No!" Larke yelled. "I won't be normal and I can't accept this because you order me to. Do you think I *liked* knowing my boyfriend was a racist, a member of a despicable hate group? I hated it. And I will always hate it."

She sniffled and wiped at a tear that fell from her lash. "You know what, maybe I'll even start hating you for telling me this. For telling me, I don't matter enough. That my feelings don't mean as much as people who are filled with hate. People who could never care about you the way I do. People who could never lo—"

"All right," he bit out, cutting her off. Chase refused to give her the chance to finish ripping his soul apart. "Hate me all you want. It's not like you loved me, anyway. Am I right?"

Maybe his approach wasn't the best but damn it, his chest felt like it was being sawed open and someone had taken a knife, carving his heart into bits and pieces. "Guess that promise of yours didn't mean shit. Staying by my side no matter what happens."

Larke shook her head hard. "I'm not the one leaving. You are. You had to have known what would happen the moment you decided to choose a bunch of racists over me. Because that is what you did. And don't for a single minute think you're doing those precious little white kids a favor. Trust me, you're now doing to them what your grandfather, mother, and stepfather did to you, helping them on the path to more hatred."

He snorted, despite the ache in his chest. "Yeah. Well, don't worry about me. Least now I know where we stand. It's cool."

Larke bit the inside of her cheek then gave him a thin smile. "You know what's funny. When I heard the knock on my door, I'd been sitting here distracted from writing because I was thinking of you."

She stopped, bit her lip and wiped at her cheek. She was silently crying now. And Chase was dying a slow agonizing death with every tear that fell. "I was thinking how badly I wanted to tell you I love you, but was afraid you wouldn't believe me. That you'd think I was saying it to make you happy. That's why I didn't tell you sooner. I wanted to wait a bit, let you see for yourself how I really felt and then when I finally told you my feelings, you'd know they were coming from inside my heart. From every single part of me, that was just madly in love with you."

Chase squeezed his eyes shut and gripped the wall behind him. His knees felt weak. He wanted to beg for forgiveness, but it was too late. His course was already set. And that was too late to change.

He glanced at Larke and watched her move to the door, holding it open. Her jaws were clenched, her eyes focused on the cream colored wall, refusing to look at him. She wanted him gone.

"Please don't make this hurt more than it already does." She was no longer wiping at the tears spilling down her cheeks. For a split second, Chase thought about saying something nasty and hurtful to offset his own pain. He couldn't. She didn't deserve it. So he did what he always did—what everyone expected of him. If Larke wanted him gone. He was gone.

Chapter Twenty

Her relationship with Chase, the man she'd begun to build her dreams around, was over. Larke cradled her face on her knees, giving in to the loud sobs racking her frame.

God. She could still see the look on his face when she'd opened the door. Betrayed. Did Chase view what happened as her abandoning him, the same way his mother had done when he was a boy? She wanted to bury her head in her hand and cry all over again.

Sniffling and wiping viciously at her eyes with a piece of the paper towel she'd grabbed from the kitchen after he'd left, Larke glanced at the printed manuscript she'd been working on. Minutes ago, sentences and phrases had been her biggest problem and now... Well now, she didn't know how she'd ever be happy again.

Chase had ripped her heart to pieces and the pain had started the moment she heard him say he couldn't walk away. Larke wrapped her arms around her stomach as a wave of nausea hit her. Why couldn't he have told her he'd changed his mind, after seeing how upset and hurt she was? What kind of love was that?

But Chase had loved her, her mind insisted. How he'd said it to her that day. Those three words had come straight from his heart. He couldn't have faked the anguish she'd heard in his voice, the hardening of his jaws as he realized he'd confessed his true feelings for her. But it still hadn't been enough. Love hadn't been enough for him to choose her.

In the days following the breakup, Larke allowed herself the time to cry and grieve. On the fourth day, with her eyes red and swollen, she forced herself to leave the comfort of her apartment and join the rest of the world outside. Mainly for cheesecake. After confessing to her friend about the breakup, Riva invited her for ice cream. The frozen treat had been another reminder of Chase so they'd settled on cake and lots of it at a local bakery and pastry shop.

As much as Larke disliked turning to food for comfort, as she'd done during childhood while dealing with her parent's divorce, it didn't impede her from eating every morsel of the cheesecake. She ordered seconds and then thirds. A shattered heart was more than enough reason to indulge, she reasoned.

Sadly, however, not even the sweetness of cake could assuage the pain or prevent her from missing Chase. Talking, being around and having him inside her. She missed it all. Without him, she was lost. Utterly lost. She hoped he felt the same without her.

Over the next two weeks, Larke was slowly able to get back into her regular routine, even managing to finish her manuscript. But once, though, in a bout of sadness, a moment of darkness, she'd broken down and called him. Chase hadn't answered on the first ring, and by the third, she'd regained her sanity and hung up.

The second time she'd contacted him was deliberate and thought out. It happened after Riva had called to ask if she'd heard what happened in Lee's Fortress. She hadn't.

Larke had grabbed up the remote and turned on the television, only to catch the end of the news segment. The last image had been of a blazing fire with smoke everywhere.

Within seconds, she'd had her phone in hand again, trying desperately to reach Chase. It was only natural that she wanted to—needed to make sure he was all right. They might not be together but that didn't mean her love for him had diminished. As before he didn't answer. Worried, Larke made it a point to call again later in the day. There was still no answer.

"If you ever call me and I don't pick up right away, it's not cause I'm ignoring you…" Chase wouldn't have ignored her then, but now? Her heart stilled at the possibilities. Either he was injured or he was ignoring her because she no longer mattered to him.

Stricken with concern and panic, Larke raced outside to her car and drove the distance to Lee's Fortress, a place she'd always made a point to avoid. The community looked the same as the last time she'd driven by with her mother many years ago.

The narrow streets were lined with houses in derelict condition, strips of paint peeling from the outside walls. Unattended gardens were overrun with weed. As she ventured deeper into the town, Larke noticed an area that was sectioned off with barricade tape from the fire department. Although the fire no longer blazed, it was clear that it had spread far enough to destroy not one but two buildings. Was one of them Chase's home? She'd never know.

Larke wasn't sure what she'd expected to find here. Maybe bystanders…one of them Chase. All she wanted was to know he hadn't been affected. That he was alive. But there was no one here. Not the one person she wanted to see.

With a heart heavy, she returned home. Alone in her apartment. Alone with the pain of not knowing.

Determined to put her mind at ease, and out of sheer desperation to hear his voice, she decided to put everything aside—pride, hurt and anger. Every single inch of her body, heart, and soul still yearned for him. Chase had become her best friend and the only person she'd ever want to be with. So, unable to do anything less, Larke held her phone, reaching out once more. Her heart sank with each and every ring that went unanswered. On the verge of hanging up, she finally heard him. Chase's voice, deep and rough, that sounded oh so sweet to her ears because it meant he was alive. He hadn't been inside the fire. But was he also safe? All right?

"Chase," she breathed. "I've tried calling you so many times."

"I know." His tone was flat. So unlike the way he normally spoke to her. "I noticed the calls."

"If you saw them, why didn't you return my calls? I know about the fire. Are you okay? Was it your house?"

"I'm fine. One of the houses belonged to Trevor." He let out a breath. "I thought we were making a clean break of it."

She gripped the phone harder, almost as if by doing so she'd be able to touch him. "You had to have known how worried I'd be."

He went silent. After a long moment, he asked, "How are you, Larke?"

Her hands shook, as well as her voice. "Not so good to be honest."

"No?"

Was he concerned? She hated no longer knowing what he thought of her.

"I miss you a lot." She squeezed her eyes shut then opened them, overcome with emotion and unable to stop herself. "I still love you, Chase and I wanted to know if you've been thinking about me. About the things I said to you."

"Yeah. I did. I've been doing a lot of thinking since we broke up. You were right to cut me loose. "

What? He hadn't even responded to the fact that she'd reminded him of her love. Swallowing back the lump in her throat, Larke held tight to the shock and hurt. "I was?"

"Yeah. It wouldn't have worked out. *We* wouldn't have worked. Things were moving too fast, anyway. We're still young. No sense in being trapped so soon."

Trapped? We were in love. I'm still in love. "Oh," she said, her voice shamefully cracking. "I um...I guess you didn't appreciate me telling you that I love you awhile ago." Her eyes began to burn. She hated crying. Wouldn't cry again. But God, they burned so much from those stupid tears trying to further her humiliation.

"Are you crying?"

She sniffled. "No." A tear broke free. She couldn't lie. "Yes. A little."

He went silent again. Larke heard nothing. Not even the sound of him breathing. For a while, she wondered if the line had gone dead. It hadn't. His next sentence, however, made her wish he'd taken pity on her and hung up without saying anything else.

"I want you to delete my number. Don't call me again."

The phone slipped from her hand as the connection ended. She covered her mouth, holding in the sob while staring at the phone. Larke cried in silence, trembling under her restraint to not allow the violent sob to break free. But the tears flowed. They refused to be contained. She wept for herself, Chase and the future they'd never have together.

He doesn't want me anymore. She shouldn't care. She shouldn't. She'd been the one to send him through the door, claiming she could no longer be with a person like him, but damn it. It hurt. So much, her stomach clenched with pain and nausea threatened to bring her to her knees. Their relationship was over. No more Chase. No more kisses. No more anything with him. She wanted to curl up into a ball and stay there forever or for however long it took to stop the hurt.

There was no going back. No apologies. No changing of mind. She'd said her piece; made her regret known and he didn't care. *Doesn't want me.* And if Chase ever decided to walk away from his hate group, he wouldn't walk freely into her arms. She wouldn't be the woman to stand with him and celebrate his freedom. That alone made her wrench her hand from her mouth, allowing the loud, god-awful cry that welled and bubbled at her throat to rip free. Uninhibited.

It took an entire month before Larke returned to life the way it was. Before she'd fallen in love and had her heart broken. Writing was going as well as could be and she'd even been invited to another book reading from a librarian who'd heard good things about her first reading. On the second go around, there were significantly less butterflies flitting around inside her stomach than the first time. Watching the smile on the faces of the children also helped to lighten her mood and provide a sense of peace.

Larke had yet to begin reading before a familiar face popped up beside her. It was the man who'd asked her out after her first reading session.

She smiled. "Did you and your daughter return to hear me read?"

The dark-haired man laughed. "No. My daughter's at her mother's house. I saw the announcement and made it a point to get here." He pulled out a copy of her book. "We forgot to ask you for an autograph the last time, do you mind?"

"No. I'd love to. What's your daughter's name?"

"Ariadne." He spelled it out.

Larke carefully signed her name then returned the book to him. "It was nice seeing you again. I appreciate—"

He interrupted. "I know I'm about to be shot down again, but would you like to go out for coffee?"

She sighed. "I told you I was in a relationship."

"That was then. What about now?"

She wanted to turn him down. Everything about this man was off. He wasn't the one she'd had her heart set on. He wasn't Chase.

Maybe that's a good thing, a voice inside her head countered. Larke hesitated and gave it some thought. Relenting, she found herself agreeing to the coffee date. She *would* put effort into forgetting Chase. Just like he'd forgotten her.

After the reading ended, they rounded a corner to a coffee shop nearby. The mid-day date was awkward at first, but after a while, Larke began to warm to him. Raymond was an architect, with a good sense of humor and they'd both grown up in the same area. It also turned out they'd even graduated from the same high school, he a few years ahead of her. That had led to some interesting conversation and jokes. But... Something was missing. There was no spark. No rush of excitement of any kind. Larke wasn't sure if she should be relieved or filled with despair.

"Tell me, how does a young lady like yourself end up writing children's books?"

She smiled. This was a safe topic. "Because I had to focus my weird imagination into

something useful."

He nodded. "Of course you know I have to ask next if your boyfriend is out of the picture?"

The smile fell. Larke stared down at her cup of coffee. "Yes, he is."

"Doesn't sound like you're happy about that. It wasn't a mutual breakup?"

This wasn't the sort of thing you discussed on a date. She knew it but still, she answered truthfully. "No. I'm not happy." She raised her head, feeling like a fool. "I'm sorry. This is weird. Not the typical thing to discuss."

Raymond shook his head. His dark eyes clouded with sympathy. "Actually no. It's not strange. I completely understand." He sipped his drink and let out a low sigh. "I'm sort of relieved you said that. You see, Larke, you're the first woman I've been attracted to in a long time. I get how you feel because I've been trying to convince myself that I'm over my ex-wife. I'm not."

"I was an experiment? A test date?" she asked, slightly hurt and feeling her ego disintegrating into ash.

"Not at all," he rushed out. "You looked so nice and seemed like a genuine person. I wanted to get to know you better. But when we're both in love with other people..."

Larke shook her head and let out a harsh laugh. What a strange situation. "Are we pathetic or just plain sad?"

Raymond quirked his thick brows. "I'd say both."

After that revelation, Larke felt more at ease, so much she accepted his invitation to catch a movie the next weekend. As friends. Which was perfect since her only good friend, Riva was on vacation.

Although Chase continued to occupy a secret part of her heart and mind, that didn't mean she had to live her life around his rejection. In no time at all, she'd be able to think of him as a fond memory. She'd be able to view her naked body and no longer recall every spot on her skin Chase had touched, kissed or licked. Bring herself to orgasm without sighing his name in throes of ecstasy.

Soon.

Chapter Twenty-One

He would never be free of Larke. That was the conclusion Chase came to, after he'd spent another night lying awake in bed replaying the sound of her voice the last time they spoke. *When I made her cry. Again.*

He hadn't meant to. Chase hadn't wanted to make her cry. But hurting Larke had been necessary. She needed to stay away from him—despise him, as she should've done from the very beginning. Which she probably did now, he thought, while waiting outside a house in a suburban neighborhood not too far from where Larke lived. Chase checked his watch, hoping any minute now the man's car would appear down the street.

It had taken a while but Chase was able to see himself for what he truly was. Knew himself to be messed up with the dirtiest kind of blood muddying his veins. Stalking Larke and now her new boyfriend–if you could call watching her a couple of times stalking–was the least of his issues.

After Trevor's death on the same night he and Larke had broken up, he'd been able to keep himself busy. He'd had to arrange the funeral while figuring out how to contact that son Trevor had mentioned. Despite Trevor's non-existent relationship with his son,

Chase knew the man had a right to know his father was no longer alive.

With his stepfather buried and gone, Chase figured he could now tackle the most important issue at hand. Larke. Mainly, the best way to tell her he was sorry and that she was right. Had been right all along. He'd never claimed to be smart, but even he should've known his expectations of Larke were unreasonable. And he had. Hours after he'd returned home from her apartment, Chase had been flooded with regret and remorse. But there was no way he could've gone to her right away.

He had to do the right thing, the only thing and make a clean break with Lee's Fortress and Antebellum Resistance. Eventually, he had. But in doing so, Chase came to realize how deep the cycle of hatred ran inside his family. This also made him realize how despicable he truly was.

How Larke could have ever found it in her to treat him so wonderful. That she could love him, left Chase stumped. He'd thought about his ignorance, the racist ideology he used to believe in. Used to, because fuck it, he was completely over hating people for being born a different race than himself. That shit was out of anyone's control and he could no longer justify any of the other white supremacist beliefs. Not when he was in love with Larke and everything about her had blown their idiotic values to dust.

As awful as it was, facing and owning up to his wrong doings, and as much as he'd wanted to plead with Larke to take him back, Chase knew it was impossible. She would never want him again. Chase knew this because there were two specific things that broke him. Made him realize with certainty that he wasn't even fit to be in the same room as the woman he loved.

After deciding to find Trevor's son, Chase had searched through the office in the small single story house used as headquarters. He'd been hoping to come across an address or phone number. He had, but he'd also stumbled upon letters and old newspaper clippings that led to him finding out a lot of things he wished he could erase from his mind.

His grandfather had written to a friend and in those letters the two men had reminisced about the people they'd attacked, harassed and pushed out of towns. They lives they'd destroyed. It had made him sick. Chase had even vomited when he'd seen the name of his father mentioned. His own father had been a filthy animal just like his twisted grandfather, participating in all kinds of violent activities.

It had taken days before he could look himself in the mirror. His entire life was a wreck. Even the ship he now owned had mostly belonged to Joseph Butler. Chase had only been able to go in on it sixty-forty with him. That meant he was profiting off the pain his grandfather had caused other people. The thought hit him hard. Especially since he couldn't do anything about that. It was his only livelihood.

And that guilt had led to even more. The weight was so heavy that the next day Chase found himself inside the sheriff's office. This was the same man who'd pulled him and Larke from the sinkhole. Chase told him about the reporter and apologized for waiting so many years to come forward with information.

"We'd always suspected your grandfather was involved. I went over there a time or two but couldn't find any solid evidence."

They wouldn't have. The Chinese man's car had been driven far away and left along the wayside. When the sheriff thanked him for the information, telling Chase the victim's widow and children would be able to put their minds to rest, he'd lost it, breaking down in front of the older man. He didn't deserve gratitude. If anything he should be locked away for withholding information.

"You were just a child," Sheriff Williams told him. "Your involvement was coerced."

Chase knew that but it didn't make him feel a single ounce better. In fact, he'd decided to be as honest as possible with the sheriff, warning the man that if he saw smoke over Lee's Fortress early in the morning, there shouldn't be a rush to put it out. Just an empty building that needed to burn. The sheriff had stared at him then gave a single jerk of the head before returning to his paperwork.

And so early the next morning, Chase had set the building on fire. As the fire blazed, he'd kept a distance, watching the flames spread to Trevor's house as the firefighters arrived and extinguished it. At one point he heard one of the firefighters say, "About fucking time this place went down in flames."

And that was that. He'd used the last of the money in the group's account to pay the IRS. Chase sold all the valuables he'd found inside the office, luxury items that Trevor had had no business buying in the first place, including a Rolex watch. He felt even more ignorant for not having taken notice of Trevor's expensive tastes.

That money along with some of his own, was used to send out the last of the stipend checks. Then he'd made the announcement, letting everyone know the experiment was over and had been a mistake and failure. He gave them instructions—stop being so terrified of the government and minorities. And then he'd left. Just like that Chase packed his pickup and drove to the lake house without sparing a single glance at the place he'd called home.

Today was no different than every day of his life spent obsessing about Larke. Who she was with and what she was doing. Twisted as he was and knowing full well that he'd never be good enough for her, Chase had driven down, all because he could no longer pretend he wasn't dying inside to have his girl back. That he wouldn't do whatever it took to have her forgiveness and trust.

He'd come to this conclusion after seeing Larke for the first time in two months last week. She'd been leaving her building wearing a black blazer over a skirt with dark tights underneath. The skirt had hugged and clung to her rounded backside and she'd left the top buttons on her blazer open, no doubt because it was too tight across her breasts. Chase bit back a groan, even now, recalling how perfect her breasts used to feel inside his hands.

At the time, she hadn't recognized him because he'd switched his red pickup for a black one with tinted windows. He'd noticed that her hair was also different. The braids were gone and as the October wind blew, her puffy curls had gathered and whipped across her face. His fingers had itched to help her tuck the unruly mass of dark coils back into place and his cock had shot so hard, wanting to thrust into her again. Thrust home. Because nothing would ever be right again unless he had her.

But he'd kept low, not alerting her to his presence. The next days had been spent carving. Working his fingers to the bone, making matching hair combs for Larke's pretty hair. After completing them, Chase returned, intent on giving the set to her, hoping she'd see the care he'd put into this gift. See that he couldn't have truly meant to hurt her or make her cry over the phone.

And that led to him waiting here, outside her new boyfriend's house. The combs, he'd ended up leaving outside her apartment door. He hadn't been able to see his plan through to hand them to her because Larke was done with him. Chase saw that he'd been beaten to the punch yesterday, after catching sight of the girl he loved coming out of her building to meet another man. A man with skin color as brown as her own and also one who apparently made her smile instead of cry then ask her to lose his number and hang up because he was a coward. A man so unlike himself.

Chase knew he only had himself to blame. But goddamn it. That fucker had his girl. Had what belonged to him. The worst was, he couldn't do a single thing about it because Larke looked happy. He wanted her happy even it meant living with the pain of having a piece of his heart missing.

Still, Chase was no saint and had easily found the boyfriend's address and now it even looked like he was rounding the corner in a sleek silver Jaguar. As soon as the man pulled up in driveway, Chase exited his truck. He was wearing a long-sleeved shirt and had made sure to make himself look real presentable, no outward sign of the white supremacist he used to be. He didn't want Larke any angrier than she would be, if the fucker went back and told her about their 'talk'. *Can't say I look like the hell I'm living in without my angel.*

The man, Raymond, as Chase had figured out, stopped as he saw Chase approach.

"Can I help you?"

"You can," Chase said, standing inches from him.

Raymond stared at him expectedly. "How? You need directions or something? Do I know you?"

"No, you don't know me. And no, I don't need directions. I'm here to talk about Larke. You're seeing her, aren't you?"

Raymond backed up, then quickly masked his brief look of panic. "What does that have to do with you?"

Before Chase could answer, Raymond shook his head and made a sound between his teeth. "Damn. You're her ex-boyfriend, aren't you?"

"She told you about me?" What would, *did* Larke tell people about him? Probably nothing good. Wasn't like he'd given her anything good to say about him.

Raymond shrugged. "Not really. My question for you is, why are you here? You and Larke are over. I just came home from the office. I don't want any trouble."

"I don't give a fuck where you just got back from. That ain't got nothing to do with what I came here for."

"Okay. Then why are you here?"

"Like I said, to have a talk with you about Larke. Didn't come to start trouble either. Unless you don't wanna listen to what I have to say, then we'll have problems."

Raymond cocked his head and folded his arms. "Yeah. All right. What is it that's so important you have to tell me? I already know everything I need to. Larke's a wonderful person."

"I know she is." Chase didn't need to hear this man tell him how wonderful Larke was. Didn't need to think about Larke smiling and being good to someone who wasn't himself. Sleeping with… Chase broke the thought. That one would kill him. *His* hands, mouth, and cock should be all she knew. He wanted to slam his fist into something. Raymond's face?

He drew in a breath, realizing he was going off the deep end. He was better, could be better than his anger. Focus. He pinned his gaze on the man who was eyeing him as if he was insane. Paying no attention to Raymond's stare, Chase remembered the importance of why he'd waited outside this house for almost an hour. "I'm here because I wanted to make sure you know how special Larke is. I knew it, but I still managed to fuck up. She got hurt because I took it for granted that she'd always be there to support me. I'm not telling you this cause I give a shit about you. I just want you to treat her like she deserves to be treated. I want her to be happy and with someone who knows her worth. So basically I'm telling you Raymond Anthony Marks." Shock immediately registered on the man's face. Chase nodded, feeling smug. "Yeah, I know every-thing about you. And trust me, you *really* don't want me to find out you've hurt Larke. Like I said, not here for trouble but for you or anyone else that fucks with her, I'll schedule my entire life around making yours a living hell. Do we understand each other?"

Raymond continued to stare at him. "If you care about Larke so much, that you're willing to stand here on my property laying out threats, why didn't you tell her all of this before? Don't you think that would've been better than being here angry because she's not yours anymore?"

Chase felt his body grow tense. "Ain't none of your business, Raymond Marks. Just remember what I said because I'm dead serious. Do *not* fuck with her." He issued the man a measured look of warning before returning to his truck. As he opened the door, Raymond shouted. "Anything else you want me to tell Larke after I let her know you've just threatened me?"

"Whatever you want, Ray. Whatever you want."

Chase slammed the door and drove off. Through his rearview

mirror, he could see the man watching him. He supposed Raymond wanted to make sure he'd really left. Soon the bastard would reach for his phone and call Larke. Raymond would speak to her the way he used to be able to talk to her. Maybe he'd even make her laugh after he told her about Chase's visit.

If Larke hadn't done so before, she'd fill him in on the bitter truth about Chase and the relationship they'd had. He would end up being the joke in their conversation. Chase groaned inside his head. The sad truth was, no matter how far he'd come with putting aside his racist views, the thought of Larke and her black boyfriend laughing at him hurt, way more than it would've if she'd taken up with another white guy. Two successful black people laughing at the trashy white boy who thought he could make her stay...

Chapter Twenty-Two

Chase had been watching her. The revelation came to Larke during a phone conversation with Raymond. When the call came a while ago, she had expected him to tell her about his evening with his ex-wife, who he was now patching things up with. The day before yesterday, she'd felt sorry for her friend and had decided to help him plan the perfect evening with the mother of his daughter. Raymond was nice and their relationship had stayed platonic.

The moment he'd informed her Chase had been waiting for him outside his house and warned him to treat her right, Larke thought her knees would buckle from under her. She'd been shocked to the core. But she'd also felt spitefully happy that Chase believed she was moving on with someone else. That feeling, however, had lasted only a few minutes. She wasn't spiteful and she didn't want to hurt him in any sort of way.

All Larke wanted was to know what Chase was thinking. Every other emotion became overshadowed by confusion. Why would he all of a sudden show concern for her, well, concern in his own crude manner?

Sighing, Larke traced her fingertips over the set of combs she'd found inside a package outside her door yesterday. Her name had been the only word written on the box. The matching combs were smooth to the touch with carefully rounded tips, that wouldn't get snagged in her hair.

At least now she knew the gift was from Chase. Had to be because of the detail. Each comb had a tree carved in the center and flying toward the tree was a bird. The bird was the only part of the comb he'd chosen to paint. Yellow and black strokes. A meadowlark bird, like her name. He'd remembered how she got her name.

Her eyes stung and her heart thundered, beating fierce against her ribcage. Did this mean Chase was still in love with her? But if he was, why hadn't he tried to contact her all this time?

And why now, when she was at her strongest since their breakup, was he tormenting her by reappearing and sending a gift? A gift he'd obviously put so much thought into.

"That guy loves you, Larke. Trust me. I can tell when a man is in love with a woman. Apart from the whole psycho threat, just the way he spoke about you, made it obvious."

Larke buried her face on her knees while trying not to allow Ray's words to play on her heart. When her heart thumped again, she knew it was too late. The beating was strong, going crazy with memories of its missing piece.

Half delirious with the need to hear his voice, Larke reached for the phone then thought better of it. Despite Chase's brutal order to delete his number, she'd never been able to bring herself to do so. Instead, she'd simply disciplined herself, knowing his number was never to be dialed.

Larke tore her gaze from the phone while contemplating her next course of action. Could she ignore what she now knew—go on with her life and allow her heart to mend or do as Chase as done? Seek him out. Her stomach flipped at the very idea. Her entire body felt wired with nerves. If Chase truly loved her then he had to be in a dark place believing she was in another relationship.

Inhaling a deep breath, Larke grabbed the two combs, neatly

arranging them in her mass of kinky curls. She grabbed her keys and made the drive to Lake Walnut. After the fire in Lee's Fortress, she'd read online that the hate group had been disbanded. Although the newspaper article hadn't gone into elaborate details, she'd shed a few tears knowing Chase was no longer involved. She'd been happy for him. And if she knew him as well as she did, then he would be at the lake house, away from it all, just him and the outdoors, waiting for hunting season to begin.

As she turned onto the street she remembered the house to be on, Larke prayed he would be there. Because if he wasn't...Lord help her, she would lose all self-respect by breaking down and calling him.

Larke released the breath she'd been holding as she approached the house. There were two vehicles parked in the driveway. A pickup she didn't recognize and a sedan. Her sweat-misted palms grew stickier. After a long moment of standing at the doorway, she gathered her courage and rang the bell.

The door opened and Larke feared her heart would break free from her chest, because Chase was standing there. He seemed bigger than life. His brown hair was slightly tousled and his blue eyes were as vivid as ever, putting the sky above to shame. Even his body seemed more powerful as if he'd been working out more.

Larke swallowed hard, suddenly wondering how she must look to him after gaining a few pounds, brought on by drowning her sorrow in food. She'd wised up and stopped but hadn't managed to lose the extra pounds yet. Damn. She shifted her feet, feeling very foolish while her entire body ached and tingled with the effort to not throw herself into his arms, then hold her face up for the kiss that always followed.

The hardening of his jaws blanketed the surprise on his face. "What are you doing here, Larke?"

Breathe. Speak. "I came to see you." *Obviously*. She tried again. "I came to see you because of yesterday. Ray told me that you said some...um...things to him about me."

His eyes darkened. "He sent you up here to talk to me?" His gaze flickered from her face to the combs in her hair but showed no reaction.

Larke shook her head. "He didn't. I came here because I wanted to. I know you were the one who left these at my door." She gestured to the combs. "They're beautiful, Chase. I love them."

He nodded, narrowing his eyes. "What does your boyfriend think about them?"

"Well, there's that. I also wanted you to know that Ray and I…" Larke stopped. There was someone behind Chase. A woman. Young. White. Thin with straight brown hair. "Chase do you mind if I…" Like herself, the girl stopped speaking, taking note of Larke's presence. Chase followed her gaze, turning around as the girl peered at Larke in surprise then mumbled something and hurried away.

Right then and there her heart died. Larke drew her eyes up to see him watching her. His entire body appeared tenser than ever. Of course. Chase wanted her gone. She, like an idiot, had convinced herself he'd been sending secret messages of his love. All she'd done was interrupt him and his girlfriend.

She wrinkled her brows, blinked away the sting in her eyes and forced the lump from her throat. "I was going to say Raymond and I are just friends. But I see it doesn't matter." She forced a smile to her lips, knowing it probably appeared wobbly. "I understand now why you wanted me to lose your number. Good reason. She's very pretty."

Oh God, she was rambling and he just stood there staring and letting her embarrass herself. Larke bit her trembling lip. "Anyway, I have a lot to do at home, so I'm just going to head on back. Sorry for disturbing you and your girlfriend. Bye."

She spun around and treaded down the driveway. One foot in front of the other, trying to hurry despite her blurred and cloudy vision caused by the tears struggling to break free. Larke could make out her car at the side of the road. All she had to do was reach the safety of inside. If she lost the battle of holding in the cry, it wouldn't matter because no one would be there to witness her pain and humiliation. To see her once and for all become undone.

Larke thought he had another girl. Chase stared at her as she hurried down the driveway. A rush of blood pounded in his eardrums. She was going to cry. That much he could tell, after she'd looked up at him with shock and hurt in her eyes. Did she think he'd left her so he could be with a certain type of girl? Chase swallowed hard. The kind of girl wasn't important, he reasoned. Not when Larke was steps away from her car and about to leave believing she'd been replaced. That was something he couldn't allow.

Chase dashed down the driveway, catching up with her as she reached the door of her car. He grabbed her hand, carefully pulling her toward him. She jerked her head, staring at him through watery eyes filled with shock and confusion.

Larke opened her mouth; maybe to question him, yell… He didn't care. Chase dipped his head, covering her lips with his own. He held tight as she began to struggle. He moved his lips, pressing it to her cheek, kissing beside her ear in the broad daylight. "She's not mine," he whispered. "That girl you just saw, she's McNair's girlfriend."

She drew back, gaping at him. "I don't understand."

"He's inside."

Larke took another step backward, her eyes rounding with fear. Chase quickly reached for her. "No. Don't do that. Don't ever be scared when I'm with you. McNair and I aren't best friends but he's not a huge ass like he was before. His girl, Abigail is Jewish. They're looking for a place together and dropped by. They're leaving soon. I promise."

"Truly?"

"Yeah. Truly." He stretched out his hand and thumbed her chin. "You look so good, angel."

"I've gained weight."

"I changed my truck. What's your point?"

She stared at him for a long pause then softened her gaze after realizing he couldn't care less about a fucking weight gain that he hadn't even noticed.

"Did you really mean what you said about only being friends with that guy?"

"Yes."

"You two never—"

"Never!" She shook her head hard. "No kiss. Nothing. You're the only man I ever want to touch or be touched by."

He nodded, feeling his chest swell with pride. Larke was his alone in every single way.

"Have you been with anyone else?" she asked quietly. It looked as if she was holding her breath. Afraid of his answer?

"No. I haven't. Don't think it'd ever feel right sleeping with anyone unless it's you."

She flattened her hand to his chest. "Then why did you tell me to leave you alone? Even after I let you know how I felt?"

"Because I felt like an idiot," he said truthfully. "I went most of my life believing and thinking some god-awful shit, when I should've known better. Then I found out about all the sick things my family did. Hurting lots of innocent people. Because I had a horrible secret that had been eating away at me since before I met you as a kid." When her eyes widened at that, he added, "I'll tell you about it, Larke. I promise. Just not right now."

She nodded. "Yes. Please do. But I don't understand why you stayed away from me because of that. I missed you so much, Chase."

"I wasn't thinking straight. Felt broken, actually. Guess, I didn't want you to waste your life with someone like me." He let out a loud breath. "I've got dirty blood running through my veins, Larke. Real dirty, fucked up blood. I figured if you ever found out the things my family did, you'd regret ever knowing me, letting me touch you."

She gazed up at him, her eyes shiny again. "I would've tried my best to help you through it. I felt awful for making you leave. I wanted to be there for you. I tried to tell you before you hung up on me, that I loved you so much and wanted to help you find a way to leave the group."

His chest swelled with pride, seeing the honesty reflected in her eyes. Chase held her close and gazed down at her. "I love you, Larke. I never stopped. Not even for a second."

"I love you too," she whispered. "I love you so much." She took his hand, bringing it to her face. In mid-action she stopped, frowning as she noticed the redness. Chase tried to draw his arm back. Larke held firm, wouldn't allow it.

"What happened?" Her vision flickered between his face and the mild swelling of his skin, where the Celtic cross was, though not as bright in color as before.

"Second bout of laser treatment."

"Because you really want them gone?"

He nodded. "The dermatologist said they might not completely fade. We're just going one at time. Planning to get them light enough so I can put new ink over them." He looked at her then. "No guarantee the laser will even work on all of them, but it's worth a try, right?"

"Yes. It is." Larke raised his hand and kissed the spot. "I hope they fade, for your sake. But it won't matter to me. I know you Chase, what's inside your heart. Everything else is unimportant."

His cheeks burned under her tender stare. He gave her a thin smile. "Thanks, angel." Clearing his throat, he glanced at the house. "Are you coming inside with me?"

She nodded, her smile bright and wide. The kind he'd missed seeing on her face. "Yes. I've been waiting for you to ask."

Chase grinned as she tucked her hand beneath his. "So if I ask you to stay here with me, you won't turn me down?"

"Depends."

He laughed. Now she sounded like him. "On what?"

She gazed at him, her eyes glinting with desire. "If we get to make love again."

He stopped in his tracks. His cock already hard, swelled, threatening to burst his pants at the seams. "Larke, it's been over two months. As soon as I get rid of McNair and his girl, I'm gonna be between your legs, licking your pussy to see if you stayed as sweet or got sweeter from missing me so much."

Her eyes fluttered close on a sigh. He stroked her cheek. "Then afterward, I'll take you from behind. Won't be nothing gentle about it, either. But you'll take it, won't you, angel?"

"I will," she said breathlessly. "Everything you give me."

His nostrils flared. "You're soaking wet, aren't you?"

She gave a single nod. "Will I have to wait long?"

God Almighty. Larke sounded as desperate as he felt, his entire body on the edge, cock straining at his pants to get to her.

"Let's go in." Chase gritted his teeth. Once he stepped through the door with Larke, McNair and his chick had better take a hint and get the fuck out.

Chapter Twenty-Three

L arke smiled inwardly as Chase dragged her behind him and through the door. Inside, she saw the "reformed psycho" McNair and the brown-haired girl standing together at a window. Both turned at the click of the door closing behind Chase.

McNair blushed with apparent embarrassment. As he should, after his disgusting behavior. Larke wasn't sure what to say with both pair of eyes on her. Chase took the task off her hands. She watched as he pinned his gaze on McNair and said in a measured tone, "You remember Larke, don't you?"

The man's face turned beet red this time. His girlfriend frowned, her eyes questioning. McNair ignored the girl's look. "Hi, Larke. Sorry about what happened in the hunting store and all."

Larke shrugged, realizing a lukewarm apology was as best as it would get. "Old news," she murmured, not accepting or declining the apology. Abigail introduced herself and she seemed nice enough. Larke figured the girl was around her age also.

"I'm glad I got a chance to meet you," Abigail said to Larke when the two women were briefly left alone. "Jesse never talked much about the group. When he suggested stopping by, I was sort of apprehensive. He mentioned that Chase wasn't like the others, but I wasn't sure. I met him today and he was polite but seeing you at the door... It was surprising and I read the look on your face when you saw me. You thought I was with Chase didn't you?"

"I did."

Abigail gave her a sympathetic smiled. "I'm really sorry about that. But I can tell you this. The Chase that I met an hour ago is different than the one who came back inside with you."

"Why do you say that?"

"He looked miserable, angry. With you he doesn't. It's dumb of me to point out since I don't really know either of you, but it was such a big difference I had to mention it." Abigail giggled then. "Kind of magical. Anyway. You guys are just really cute together and I wanted to wish you happiness."

"Thank you, Abigail," Larke said, meaning it from the bottom of her heart, because she *did* feel magical.

When she was finally alone with Chase as McNair's car rolled out of the driveway, Larke thought about her very first encounter with him. Perhaps they'd always been destined for each other. Her panicking on the bus and getting off at Lee's Fortress of all places then coming upon Chase only to land in a sinkhole with him. Were they *forced* together? Did some higher power know the only way she could've found her way inside his hardened prejudiced heart was for him to have a memory of kindness that had been untainted?

Larke chose to believe so. Her and Chase were perfect together. She sighed as she followed him into the bedroom. Her stomach tangled into knots when his voice, deep and rich hit her ears, making her dizzy.

"Come to me." Chase stood beside the bed, his gaze intense and pinned on her.

Larke reached him, raising her head for his kiss. *I'm drunk with lust.* Her knees went weak and her head spun as he squeezed her waist, holding her tight to his erection.

Breaking free of the kiss, Larke traced a path with her lips from his jaw to his neck. With a ragged breath, Chase gently pushed her away then grated, "Take off your clothes," while jerking the shirt over his head.

Fumbling to remove her clothes, Larke bit back a moan, watching Chase remove his pants and boxers. Oh God. She released a cry at the sight of his penis, big and hard stretching toward her. The crown was red, engorged and glistening with juices. She stepped out of her underwear and dropped to the floor in front of him, unable to think.

Just want to lick. Taste him. Suck. Larke looked up at Chase, then down at his cock, feeling wetness seeping from her mouth. She licked her lips and pushed her head forward, closing her mouth around the slickened crown. Salty pre-cum hit her tongue like a decadent treat, causing her to moan in the back of her throat. Oh my God. How she had missed this! Larke suckled hard, drawing on the slit, pulling, pulling and…

She heard a hoarse yell, felt her head being jerked backward. His penis slipped from between her lips. Her mouth was empty. "No," she whimpered, tossing her head from his grasp. He'd tasted so good.

"Larke!" Chase was peering down at her. His hand stroked the tip of his cock and his massive chest rose and fell with effort. She stared at him in confusion. "Why did you make me stop?"

Groaning, he took her hand, helping her off the floor. "I told you I wanted to lick your pussy. I'm going crazy here. I gotta taste you now. It's been too long. Get on the bed and you can keep sucking my dick. We can do both."

Her body shivered. Of course. They'd done so before. Nodding, Larke climbed on the bed, lying sideways with her head facing the edge. When Chase joined her, she threw her leg over his shoulder, felt his hand dig into her flesh as his tongue lashed between her labia. Her mouth opened on a cry then lowered, closing around his thick shaft. Over and over she suckled, lapping at the tip and laving her tongue up and down his length. Her hips bucked and her body shivered from the feel of his mouth on her pussy.

In response, Larke brought his penis to the back of her throat and held him there. She moaned inside her head as jets of semen arced from his cock, wetting the passage of her throat. Swallowing quickly, Larke felt her entire body tremble from the tongue working her pussy, bringing her to orgasm.

The sound of her own erratic breathing thrummed in her eardrum. Larke raised her head. She stared at Chase while bringing her legs together. He rolled to his back and crooked his finger. She was beside him in an instant, resting her head on his shoulder.

"Same as always?"

His lips slanted into a grin. "Better. Sweeter. Think I tasted candy this time." He turned and grabbed her around the waist. "Is that what you've been eating all this time, cookies, cakes and everything sweet?"

Larke grinned, knowing he was playing. "I had to find a replacement for you," she murmured, biting her lip as he cupped her ass and squeezed.

"How did that work out?" He shifted his attention to her breast, lowering his head to capture a nipple and suck.

"N-not so good. No replacement for you."

"Hmm." He kept sucking at her nipple, stroking her belly. Releasing a sigh, Larke closed her eyes and raked her fingers through his hair, reveling in the feel of his mouth on her breast.

After several minutes, Chase lifted his head. Larke immediately recognized the glint in his eyes. Felt the hardness of his cock prodding against her thigh. "Remember what I said to you outside?" he asked huskily.

She nodded, swallowing hard while casting her gaze downward. Chase was more than ready to make good on his promise.

When he spoke next, it was a terse order. "Hold on to the edge of the bed and open up for me."

Larke did just that. Hands gripping the bed, she heard the sound of her own cry, something between a whimper of pain and a moan of utter bliss as Chase rammed the length of his cock into her from behind. Craning her neck, she stared at the man pumping deep inside her, his tall, muscular frame, taut with every stroke, pounding at her walls. Her body cried, strung out on pleasure and her heart thumped, beating with love. So much love for Chase and gratitude to whatever power played a role into turning the mayhem of their first encounter into what she knew would be a lifetime of love.

Epilogue

Five Years Later

Chase glanced down at his four-year-old daughter, Alicia. The little girl was sitting on the floor of his workroom, which also doubled as an office. Although he'd been lucky enough to add two more ships to his cargo shipping business, and was focused on making the business even more of a success than it already was, he still found time here and there to work on his hobby. Carving, it seemed was also a hobby his little girl enjoyed as much as he did. Maybe a bit too much, Chase thought as he looked down again from his chair to see her digging, or rather, try to dig the dull knife he'd given her, into a piece of wood. He shook his head, taking note of her face scrunching up as she pushed away a curl that had loosened from her hair clip.

"What's wrong?" he asked, knowing she would continue on like this until he said something.

She immediately dropped the knife and let out a dramatic sigh. Chase bit back his smile. This was serious matter if she was sighing like that. Alicia burst into a long, drawn-out tale about a boy in her pre-school class, who was being mean to her and some other kids.

"Did you ask him to play with you?"

She fingered Larke's old necklace, which she insisted on wearing every single day. "Yes. He kicked the game and laughed." She folded her arms and pursed her lips. "I hate him."

"You don't hate anyone," Chase told her. He lifted her in his arms and seated her across his lap. "How about this—next time this kid is mean to you, just try to be nice. Give it a couple of tries."

She stared at him as if he was crazy. "No."

Chase groaned inside his head. The kid was way too stubborn for her own good. He let out a breath. "All right, why not?"

"He's dumb. Won't be my friend."

"Alicia, you don't know that. Plus, I'm the adult so I know more than you about these things."

She narrowed her brown eyes at him. "You do?"

He nodded and gave her a squeeze. God, the little thing looked so much like Larke. "Yeah I do," he answered. His throat suddenly felt tight as he spoke. "When I was a kid, I wasn't very nice to mommy when she wanted to be my friend."

Alicia's eyes widened. She scrunched up her face again, frowning. "B-but, you're so nice, daddy." She rubbed her cheek against his then kissed him. "You're the nicest daddy in the world."

Chase chuckled. "Thanks, baby. Anyway, my point is, all you gotta do is try and be nice. Might not work, but at least you gave it a shot."

She pushed her lips to the side, concentrating hard. Finally, her little face relaxed as she nodded. "Mommy would do that too."

"She would." And Larke had. Treating him with kindness and love. Being his everything. Chase lifted his daughter off his lap and set her on her feet. "Now hurry up and go put on your jacket and boots."

Reminded of their planned walk through the park, Alicia hurried out of the room without hesitation. It was late May in Juneau, the city he and Larke had moved to months after they'd gotten back together and he'd sold the lake house. When he'd asked Larke to marry him one night as they'd lain in bed together, she'd shouted yes and thrown herself into his arms so hard, causing both of them to roll right off the bed, landing on the floor in a tangled heap. And when he'd told her of his wish for the two of them to live away from the hustle and bustle, she hadn't hesitated when he'd suggested a mountainous area of Alaska. Had even exclaimed that such a place might provide all the inspiration she needed for her ever-growing list of published books.

He stepped out of his office and saw Larke heading his way. Behind her was their two-year-old son Ronan, running toward the living room. Chase ruffled the boy's hair as he whizzed by. It was obvious he needed to beat his sister as the first to the door.

"Those two are insane," Larke said, shaking her head as Alicia came racing down the hallway, shouting that Ronan had tricked her into losing.

"You mean like you," Chase said, wrapping his arm around his wife's waist. Larke swatted his arm, half-heartedly squirming out of his hold.

"Stop moving around," he whispered, clasping her tighter to him. She looked up, lowered her lashes then grinned, real smug. Larke knew the power she had over him. Knew it and used it to her advantage, which he didn't really mind because it always ended in both of them being satisfied and pleasured out of their minds.

Larke raised her face and pressed her lips to his. "It's a good thing we're going out in the cold then."

Chase raised his brows. "It is?"

"Yes. Because when we come back in after such a long walk, the children will be tired and…"

He swallowed hard, gazing down at her. "I can warm you up."

She smiled. "Yes. We can warm each other."

Chase nodded while blocking out the sound of the kids calling to them. He loved his children to death, but nothing was going to stop him from taking the time he wanted to simply stare at his wife, awing over the fact she was his. Larke was his best friend, the one person who knew him inside out and accepted him exactly as he was.

When some of the tattoos hadn't faded as much as he would've liked, she'd comforted him, reminding him of how far they'd come and that in the big scheme of things, the symbols no longer had meaning. They'd both decided when the children asked, they'd tell the entire story of Chase's past and use it as a teaching lesson to make sure their children always remained open-minded, not just about other people but life in general.

Speaking of… Chase traced his thumb along Larke's cheek. She was three months pregnant and it would only be a matter of time before their daughter started asking questions. "Do you think we should tell the kids when we go out?"

Larke drew in a deep breath. "Ronan won't understand, but I hope Alicia is excited."

He snorted. "She will be, if we do it inside an ice-cream shop."

Larke laughed and laid her head on his chest. "I think you're the one who one wants ice-cream but keep pretending it's our little girl."

Chase cupped the back of her head and gently lifted it from his chest, forcing her to meet his eyes. "Maybe. But you forget, angel. You're still the sweetest thing I ever had or tasted." He kissed her then. "I love you, Larke."

"I love you too," she murmured. "I'll always love you, Chase."

He grinned at her as they turned their heads to see their two kids staring at them. Alicia had her head cocked to the side with a funny grin on her face. Ronan was beside her, making a sour face. "You guys kiss too much," Alicia said, making a face to rival her brother's.

Letting out a low growl, Chase scooped his daughter up in his arms and started kissing her face. She giggled and twisted in his arms. Soon, he handed her over to Larke, who did the same, while he turned Ronan sideways in his arms, covering the toddler's face with kisses. The little boy wriggled his way to rest his head on Chase's shoulder. He sighed and said, "Daddy, I love you."

And just like that, his heart expanded and his life felt completed, filled with happiness. With Larke he'd found everything and more than he'd ever dreamed of having. Life was all good.

About the Author

Delilah Hunt lives in Germany with her husband and three children. From the moment she opened her first romance novel at the tender age of twelve, she has never looked back, holding this genre close to her heart. Apart from writing and reading, Delilah Hunt loves to be outside, going for long walks and getting ideas for her next books.

If you enjoyed this book and any of her other books, please be sure to leave a review and stop by her site at www.delilahhunt.com to see what else she is working on. Thank you.

Printed in Great Britain
by Amazon

19113230R00139